MAIL-ORDER BRIDE
WESTWARD BOUND

MONTANA MAIL-ORDER BRIDES BOOK 3

LINDA BRIDEY

This book is dedicated to all of my faithful readers, without whom I would be nothing. I thank you for the support, reviews, love, and friendship you have shown me as we have gone through this journey together. I am truly blessed to have such a wonderful readership.

CONTENTS

CHARACTER LIST

Marcus Samuels
> **Claire O'Connor**
> Seth & Maddie Samuels, rancher and wife
> Tessa & Dean Samuels, rancher and wife. Children: Jack, Sadie, & Michael
> Tucker Foster, Sadie's boyfriend
> Lydia & Charlie Benson, neighbors of the Samuels
> Maureen O'Connor, Claire's mother
> Geoffrey O'Connor, Claire's father
> Mrs. Duncan, head housekeeper at the O'Connor house
> Black Fox & Wind Spirit, Lakota brave and wife. Children: Raven & Winona
> He Who Runs, Lakota brave
> Owl, Lakota brave
> Aiyana, Marcus's daughter
> Redtail, Aiyana's mother (deceased)
> Marty & Ray, cattle drivers
> Dr. Turner, doctor
> John Williams, circuit preacher

CHAPTER 1

A bitter wind blew the snow into mini-tornados that danced across the pastures of the Samuels ranch. At eight below zero, working outside was torture so only the most essential chores got done, like feeding the stock and cleaning stalls. Dean and Seth Samuels had moved their herds closer to home so they could check on them and make sure they didn't freeze at night. They needed to make them move at night to keep their blood warm.

At that time of year, few calves were born, but several cows had already given birth and the Samuels brothers had penned them in a covered enclosure to keep them warm and dry. Marcus, the youngest, slept during the day because he was the one out at night moving the herds around. He was a night owl and had no trouble keeping awake, unlike his brothers, who usually preferred to go to bed fairly early.

Dean and Seth also minded the cold more than he did. Especially Seth, who had been badly injured on a cattle drive three years previously. His right leg had been damaged almost beyond repair. If it hadn't been for his wife's father taking him to Pittsburgh for surgery, he would have lost the leg.

The surgeon had been able to save it by attaching metal rods to the broken thigh and calf bones. The ligaments in his leg had also been repaired. His recovery had been slow, but he was almost as good as new now. Still, Seth had trouble dealing with frigid temperatures because arthritis had settled in the leg. He also experienced more pain in the leg at night.

Marcus liked watching the snow move over the landscape under the moonlight, and he smiled as the snow swirled ever higher until it blocked some of the stars from view. He'd left Rosie, his palomino mare, in the barn because it was so cold out. They'd recently had a blizzard that had dumped almost two feet of snow on them, and the going was a little rough for the horses. Marcus didn't need a horse to move the herds around; he was perfectly happy to use his snowshoes.

He danced around the pasture to keep warm, but also because he enjoyed it. His wolfskin coat and fur-lined boots kept the worst of the wind out, and the matching hood protected his ears and face from frostbite. The snowshoes kept him from sinking too deep into the snow, allowing him to move quickly when needed.

As he danced, Roscoe, his big, hairy wolf-dog, playfully attacked him and Marcus went down face-first into the snow. Instead of getting angry, he laughed and rolled over to face the "vicious" dog that snapped his inch-and-a-half long fangs close to his throat. To anyone else, it would have appeared that the dog was seriously intent on killing the man.

Marcus, however, knew that Roscoe was only playing around. He hurled the dog from him and jumped up. As soon as he regained his balance, he took off running. It was time to roust the steers, and he figured he could have some fun at the same time. A few of the beasts were lying down. Marcus ran over to the closest one, jumped on its back, and thumped its sides with his gloved hands.

The poor steer was startled and rose as quickly as it could. Marcus jumped clear and headed for the next one. Roscoe didn't accompany him. The dog had had some bad experiences with cattle and wouldn't come near them. He guarded them, but he wouldn't herd them like Jasper or Belle, the collies. Marcus whistled a happy tune as he went about his work. When he had the steers up and moving, he hopped the fence and did the same with the heifers and cows. During the summer when the footing was sure, Marcus could run rings around the bulls, but he didn't mess with them when there was a chance that he could slip. If he went down, he would most likely not get up again. He had no desire to be gored to death.

He sent Jasper to move them instead. He'd noticed that Jasper was moving a little slower than usual and thought he'd voice his concerns again to Dean. Jasper was almost twelve, and Marcus kept telling his brother that it was time to keep a couple of the puppies that Jasper and Belle produced to replace the older dogs. He whistled to Jasper to come in, and the dog turned away from the longhorn and started back to him. The bull started chasing the dog, and Marcus knew Jasper wasn't going to make it out in time.

Marcus swore and jumped the fence. The movement distracted the bull, and it turned in Marcus's direction instead. Marcus kept yelling until Jasper was clear, then he jumped back over the fence.

When first light came, he whistled to the dogs and marched toward Dean and Tessa's house. He saw the light in the kitchen windows and knew that Dean would be eating his breakfast before starting his day.

He slipped through the fence and crossed the drive to the house. At the porch, he stopped long enough to take off his snowshoes and toss them aside, then continued on his way. Roscoe tried to follow, but Marcus made him wait outside on the porch.

Dean was startled when the door banged open. He jerked and slopped coffee onto the table. Angrily, he looked at Marcus and said, "What's the matter with you?"

Marcus motioned for Jasper to come into the house, then slammed the door shut. He pointed at Jasper. "Do you love this dog?"

"What?"

"Yes or no; do you love this dog?" Marcus asked again.

Dean didn't know what Marcus was getting at, but he could tell that his britches were twisted up about something. "Yes. Why?"

Marcus took off his coat and hung it on the back of a chair. He went to the stove, poured a cup of coffee from the kettle on it, and sat down before he answered.

"If you love Jasper and you'd like to keep him around for a while longer, I'd suggest you retire him. He's not up to the job anymore, Dean."

Dean let out a snort of derision. "You don't know what you're talking about, Marcus."

"The heck I don't! I just had to save his skin from Thumper out there. If I hadn't distracted that bull, Jasper wouldn't be sitting here right now. He's not as quick as he used to be and his hearing is starting to go. I've seen it with my own eyes," Marcus explained willfully. "When are you going to accept it and keep some pups for Jasper and Belle to help train? We're growing and we need more cattle dogs, anyway."

He took a swig of the hot coffee and felt it warm him all the way to his toes. From the way Dean was looking at him, he could tell that his brother was taking him seriously.

Dean knew that Marcus could sometimes be melodramatic. But when he acted like this, he meant business. "Okay. Maybe it is time," he said, stroking Jasper's silky head. "Good thing we've got a litter on the way. They'll be ready to start training up by spring."

"Thank you," Marcus said. Mollified, his mood improved immediately. "What's for breakfast?"

"Eggs, toast, and bacon."

Marcus rubbed his hands together in anticipation and then stopped. "So how come I don't smell any?"

Dean smiled at him. "Because you have to make them."

"What? I just worked all night and now I have to cook, too? Why don't you cook?"

"Do you really want me to make the eggs?" Dean asked, cocking his head.

"No. Your eggs stink. Tessa still having bad morning sickness, huh?" Marcus asked. He felt bad for his sister-in-law. This pregnancy was a little more volatile than when she'd carried Mikey.

Nodding, Dean downed the last of his coffee and stood. "Yeah, she can't stand the smell of food this early. So, come on and help me out so I can get started outside, please?"

"All right," Marcus said good-naturedly. "Since you asked nicely. Wait, where's Sadie?"

"Over at Lydia's. She stayed over there last night."

Marcus saw Dean's jaw tighten and regretted bringing up his niece's name. Sadie and Dean had been butting heads of late, and there were times when Sadie stayed with their friends down the road. "Sorry, Dean."

Dean just nodded. The kitchen door opened again and Seth came through the doorway, bringing cold air with him. He shut the door quickly. "Are you cookin'?" he asked Marcus.

Marcus frowned at him. "Didn't Maddie cook?"

"Yes, and I ate it, but I could use a little something else," Seth replied.

Maddie hadn't mastered the art of cooking ranch food, even after being there for three years. She tried valiantly, but it didn't seem as though she'd ever really get the knack. Seth ate almost everything she cooked because he didn't want to make her feel worse about it than she did. But more often than not, it didn't fill him up.

Marcus laughed and jumped up from the table and set about making the meal. As he worked, his brothers watched his quick movements with amusement and admiration. He whistled a tune as he flipped the eggs without using a spatula and tended the bacon. When the food was almost done, he told Dean to go get the boys.

He'd barely set a plate of steaming eggs, bacon, home fries, and toast down in front of Seth before his eldest brother attacked it like he hadn't eaten in a week.

Dean went to the foot of the stairs and collided with his son Jack, who was on his way to the kitchen. Jack was clearly in a hurry, and Dean figured it was because he was hungry and had smelled the food cooking. Eating was probably the most important activity in Jack's life. Now thirteen years old, he was only a foot shorter than Dean and a carbon copy of his father.

"Oh, sorry, Pa. I didn't know you were there," Jack said with a smile. "Mikey's still sleeping. I just let him be."

"You're getting so big you almost knocked me down," Dean said, ruffling his son's hair.

Dean and Sadie might not be getting along, but Jack was as close to his father as ever. Jack was old enough to work on the ranch now and helped out quite a bit. Dean usually had him do simple duties like clean stalls and feed the stock. He knew the boy was itching to go on a cattle drive, but Jack was still too young.

Jack sat down at the kitchen table. "Mornin', Uncles. Is Mama still in bed?"

Seth said, "Yep. Still can't hack food in the morning."

"That's a shame. This baby's doing a number on her. Must be a girl," Jack said with a grin.

Marcus placed a full plate in front of him, and the boy tucked into it with as much gusto as Seth had. Jack had always had a voracious appetite. There were times when Dean's first wife had run out of milk when she was still breastfeeding and they'd had to supplement with cow's milk. Baby Jack hadn't minded, and he was now a big, strong teenager. Although he looked like Dean, he had Sarah's gentler nature and was an excellent babysitter to his five-year-old brother, Mikey.

Marcus served Dean and then started mixing something in a pan. He added water and several different spices and heated the mixture. When Marcus was satisfied that it was heated through, he put it in a cup and placed it in front of Dean.

"What's that?" Dean asked.

"Let it cool and give it to your wife. It'll help settle her stomach," Marcus replied.

Dean picked up the cup and sniffed the concoction. "God, that smells awful," he said and made a face.

"I know, but it'll fix her right up. Trust me."

"Where do you learn this stuff?" Seth asked.

Marcus thought fast. There was no way he could tell them the truth about the origins of the potion. "In some of those college books that Claire keeps sending me."

Seth accepted his answer with a nod and swallowed a bite of bacon. "Speaking of Claire, she sent you another letter." He fished it from the front pocket of his coat that was hanging on the back of his chair.

Marcus sighed and put a hand to his head. "What is it with her?"

"She likes you," Dean said.

"No, she doesn't," Marcus protested. "She likes to bug the heck out of me. We have this long-distance argument going on. She just won't quit."

"Like you told me six years ago, you didn't have to answer her letters," Dean pointed out.

"That's the problem; I really don't have a choice. If I don't answer her, everyone will get mad at me. Especially him," Marcus said, pointing at Seth.

"That's right. She's a sweet, smart girl and you oughta be nice to her," Seth said. He had become very close with Claire when he'd stayed with the O'Connors in Pittsburgh. Now he thought of her as a little sister.

Marcus scowled. "Maybe she's sweet to you, but she's never been nice to me, whether it's in person or in her letters. She's condescending, argumentative, and just an all-around pain in the neck. The only good thing about writing back and forth with her is that she sends me those books."

"You know why she does that, right?" Dean asked.

"Why?"

"To make sure you can keep up with her so you can keep the debate going."

Marcus stopped chewing, and his gray eyes widened in surprise.

Seth laughed. "Marcus, for all your brains, you sure have a hard time figuring out women."

"I don't *normally* have a problem with women. She's just too complicated. I like my women simpler," Marcus replied.

"How come we never meet these women?" Dean asked.

Marcus shrugged. "I'm not seeing anyone on a regular basis, so there's no need for you to meet them."

"I remember the days of seeing more than one woman, Marcus," Seth said. "I'm glad they're over."

It was easy to see how much in love Maddie and Seth were. The only disappointment in their life together was that Maddie hadn't conceived a child thus far. She and Seth wanted children in the worst way, but it just hadn't happened yet.

Marcus got up and put his plate in the sink as Seth left. He was about to start heating the water to wash the breakfast dishes so Tessa didn't have to do it later when Dean stopped him.

"You've done enough. Sadie can clean up when she gets home. Charlie said he'd have her home by eight, so she won't be too long now."

"Okay," Marcus said. "I guess that means I'm headed home to bed." He started putting on his wolfskin coat.

"I'd like to have one of those," Dean said, eying it appreciatively.

"I'll keep that in mind," Marcus said. "Remember what I said about Jasper." He put a hand on Jack's shoulder and said, "See ya, kid."

ONCE HOME, Marcus put Rosie away and fed her and his other horse, Arrow. He also owned a mule named Bucky, a few chickens, and several steers. He collected a couple of eggs that the chickens had left him and went inside.

Compared to Dean and Seth's places, it was small. There were only four rooms; a kitchen, a small parlor, a bedroom, and a tiny washroom. Most of the surfaces were piled high with books, and rough-hewn bookcases lined many of the walls. It was cold because there'd been no fire overnight, so Marcus didn't take off his coat. He got fires going in the kitchen stove and the fireplace in the parlor.

With a grimace, he pulled Claire's letter from his coat pocket and tossed it on the table. He had to admit that Claire had very nice handwriting and his name and address were very clear. Since it would be a little while before the house heated up and he didn't want to get into a cold bed, he decided to read it and sat at the kitchen table near the stove. He slit the envelope with a penknife and opened it.

Dear Marcus,

I hope this letter finds you well. I'm very excited to tell you that this is my last semester at college and I will graduate at the end of May, two months from now.

"Like I don't know that May is two months from now," Marcus mumbled.

The time has flown by, and while I'm happy to be earning a college diploma, I'm also a little sad that it will be over.

"That's it, Claire. Rub my face in the fact that I never went to college," Marcus muttered. Seth couldn't see it, but behind her seemingly innocent words was a whole other meaning.

I would love for my sisters to attend the graduation ceremony, but I doubt that Tessa will feel up to traveling such a long distance when she is six months along. I'm sure that Maddie and Seth will come, but I know that if they do, it means that you will have to stay to help with the ranch.

Which really means that she's glad I'll be staying home, Marcus thought. That did bother him a little because he would like to visit a college and see a graduation ceremony.

Mama and Papa send their regards to you. They are very anxious for August to come so they can meet their newest grandchild. When we come to visit, would it be possible for you to not flirt with Mama so much? It's very unseemly and bothers Papa so.

Marcus's smile was vicious. "You think it's been bad before? Just you wait. You haven't seen *unseemly*, little girl. Geoffrey's a grown man and he can take it."

I hope you're enjoying the last package of books I sent you. I'm sure you'll learn many new things from them. There are a lot of new scientific theories discussed, such as Gregor Mendel's laws of heredity. Did you get to that particular subject? If so, what are your thoughts on it? I particularly found the studies he performed on the inheritance patterns of garden peas fascinating.

"Garden peas?" Marcus muttered. "He studied the heredity of garden peas? This I gotta see, but not right now."

The house was toasty by then, and Marcus was getting sleepy. He threw his coat on the small sofa in the parlor and slipped off his boots. He left a trail of clothes on his way to his bedroom and fell into bed.

CHAPTER 2

*C*laire O'Connor was going over some financial ledgers with her father in his study. Geoffrey had found a few discrepancies in one of the shipping accounts and wanted his daughter's thoughts on where they had happened. Claire preferred to stretch out on the floor to work rather than sit at a desk.

Papers and ledgers were spread around her as she worked. She lay on her stomach, bending her legs up and down, a sign that she was deep in concentration. Geoffrey was getting nowhere with the ledgers he was looking at. Everything in them was spot on and added up, yet there was money missing. He took off his new pair of glasses, rubbed his tired eyes, and leaned back in his chair for a moment.

"Papa!"

Geoffrey jumped at Claire's excited cry. He leaned forward again and opened his eyes.

"What is it?"

Claire plunked a ledger down in front of him and pointed at one of the entries. "Look! Someone has altered these two figures here."

Geoffrey put his glasses back on. He hated wearing them, but sometimes it was necessary. They made him feel like an old man, but Maureen told him they made him look very distinguished. He looked where Claire had pointed and saw what she meant. The changed numbers added up to $2,178; a nice sum, indeed.

Geoffrey stood up abruptly and began pacing back and forth. This wasn't the first time it had happened, but he intended for it to be the last. "Thank you, Claire."

Claire knew exactly what this meant and was just as angry as her father. "Papa, we have to find out who is behind this. It cannot continue."

Geoffrey stopped his pacing. "No, Claire, *I* have to find out who's doing this. But you are correct; it must be stopped."

"Why don't you want me to help you?" Claire asked. "Together, we would be able to get to the bottom of it rapidly."

"While I don't doubt that, should it go to court, you would have to testify, and I don't want that for you," Geoffrey explained.

Claire's temper flared. "I can take care of myself and I wouldn't mind testifying if it meant whoever the culprit is would be punished."

"I appreciate that, Claire, but my decision stands. I thank you for your assistance as always, but I'll take it from here," Geoffrey said.

Claire drew herself to her full height, and Geoffrey knew he was in for a tongue-lashing. "I fail to see why it is that I'm good enough to help find the discrepancy but not to help find the guilty party. I would be a valuable asset in doing so since I know your employees. They consider me a child, as you do apparently, and do not see me as a threat. They might let something slip when they think I'm not listening. Do as you wish, Papa. However, I will not be offering any more assistance."

"You know how much I appreciate your help, but I will not let you play at investigating. It could become dangerous, and I'll not have another daughter hurt or worse," Geoffrey countered. He was referring to her sister Maddie being attacked by a former friend of the family several years ago. "If you become angry with me, so be it. The subject is closed. And do not think that being cool with me will change my mind. I'll not have it. Do you understand, Claire?"

A little of the fight went out of Claire. "Very well, Papa. I won't be cool with you, but I still am not going to assist any longer. I think you are being chauvinistic."

Geoffrey's eyebrows shot up. "Chauvinistic? Me? I have three daughters of whom I am very proud. How could I possibly be chauvinistic?"

Claire's chin rose, and her cinnamon-colored eyes met his. "Can you honestly tell me that you wouldn't let me help you more if I were your son instead of your daughter?"

Geoffrey was ashamed to admit she was right, but he felt justified after what had happened to Maddie. "Perhaps I am a trifle chauvinistic after all, Claire, but for good reasons, as you well know."

"All right, I can understand your reasoning for not wanting me to play detective, but why will you not consider hiring me and letting me work with you? You know I would be useful and I would work harder than anyone else. If I was your son, you would have already been grooming me to take over when you decided to step down," Claire said.

Geoffrey realized that this was what she'd been getting around to all along. He hated it when she was able to trick him, and she did it often. She'd bested him again. "I concede your point, Claire. Again, this is for your protection. Do you really think that you would be treated fairly by your superiors? If I had a son, I would have made him start at the bottom and work his way up like everyone else. I would constantly have to run interference for you. Would you want that?"

"Do you have to run interference for me right now, Papa?" Claire asked in return.

Geoffrey was incensed by this point. "No, daughter. You are correct. In a lot of instances, you are perfectly capable of outwitting many people, including myself, but this is my company and I am standing by my decision. Call me chauvinistic if you like, but that's my final word on the subject."

Claire's delicate jaw worked as she fought back tears. She would not cry. "Fine. Then we are agreed. It is *your* company and I am *not* an employee. I stand by *my* decision in that I will no longer be helping you in your business matters. Unless you would like to hire me as a consultant. Should you want to do that in the future, we would need to discuss the terms and my payment. Have a pleasant evening, Papa." With her point made, she left the study.

Geoffrey stared after her for several minutes. While Tessa and Maddie had not been easy to deal with at times, Claire could be a nightmare because of her brilliant mind. One minute she was the sweetest, most lovable young woman, and then the next moment a formidable and infuriating creature.

He looked down at the floor and realized that she'd left without cleaning up her mess. Angrily, he began picking up the ledgers and papers.

AFTER LEAVING THE STUDY, Claire found her mother in the parlor. "Good evening, Mama," she said.

"Hello, Claire. Are you finished helping your father?"

"Yes, I am quite finished helping Papa, this evening and any other," Claire stated.

"What do you mean?" Maureen asked with concern in her blue eyes.

"I might as well let you know that he and I are having a difference of opinion, so I will leave him to his business and not be involved in it any longer."

Maureen gave Claire an admonishing look. "Claire, what kind of attitude is that to have toward him?"

"Mama, you don't understand. I help him all the time. I help with the accounts, with correspondence, and with anything else he has ever asked me to do. Yet, he will not even entertain the notion that I should be groomed to take over one day. He does not trust me enough to be strong enough to do so. My labors are fruitless. I should have been born a boy. If I had, he would want me to work with him." She paused and took a deep breath. "I'm sorry, Mama, but that is the way I feel. I am going to bed." She kissed her mother and left the room.

"There's a letter from Marcus on the table in the foyer!" Maureen called after her.

Claire skidded to a stop and backtracked to the table. She smiled as she picked up the letter and ran up the stairs to her room. After closing her door, she jumped onto her bed to read the letter.

My Dearest Claire,

She narrowed her eyes. This was not an auspicious beginning. She knew she was anything *but* his dearest anything.

I'm doing quite well. It's very cold here right now. We had a blizzard about a week ago, so the snow is very deep. I stay outside all night moving the herds every so often so they don't freeze to death. It's hard work, but it must be done.

"Another jab that I don't work," Claire muttered. She thought about her father's decision and realized that Marcus's barb had hit its mark.

I congratulate you on your upcoming graduation. Just keep doing what you're doing and you'll actually make it.

That statement made Claire sit up. She was seething with fury at his insult.

It's okay if I can't come to the ceremony. I know how close you are to Maddie and Seth, so I'm only too happy to take over for Seth while he's gone. Tell me, does Maddie know how attached you are to my brother?

"Oh! How dare he?" Claire shouted.

The books are very informative and I thank you for sending them. I'm pretty much through with them, however. I look forward to receiving the next ones. Of course, there won't be any more after May. Perhaps one of your male classmates who is going on to medical or legal school wouldn't mind donating some to me?

Her anger reached new levels. He was making fun of her for not being able to study for another degree since there were no schools in Pittsburgh that accepted women applicants for doctorate programs.

Now on to these studies by Mendel...

Claire read his observations and his challenges to her views, composing her responses even as she read. As soon as she'd finished reading his letter, she grabbed a pen and some paper and sat down to write back. She meant to refute his points on heredity and come back with cutting insults, but that wasn't what came out. Instead, she wrote an angry composition that basically called him and every other male a chauvinist.

She didn't realize it, but angry tears dripped down her face and landed on the paper. They were still there when she folded the letter and put it in the envelope. She addressed it and went downstairs to put it with the other outgoing mail.

Geoffrey was coming out of his study as she stomped across the foyer to the table and slapped the letter down in the mail basket. She turned, saw her father and gave him a look filled with cold fury, and stomped back upstairs.

"Who else has gotten on her bad side?" he wondered as he walked over to the table. He saw Marcus's name on the envelope and wondered what he'd done to upset her. That she was angry at someone besides him made him feel better. He was very curious about what the letter contained, but he wouldn't intrude upon her privacy. He had no interest in compounding his predicament by doing such a thing.

CHAPTER 3

A week later, Marcus was once again cooking breakfast. He turned around from the stove, saw Seth take a letter out of his coat, and leaped forward and snatched the letter from Seth's fingers before he'd barely gotten it clear.

"Hey!" Seth objected.

Marcus looked at him with glee. "I've been waiting on this," he said.

"You have? I thought you hated getting Claire's letters."

"I do."

"But you're happy this one came?"

"Yeah."

"I'm confused. It's too early in the morning for your mood swings, Marcus," Seth said as he sat down.

"Your leg isn't broken anymore, Seth. Get your food yourself. I wanna read this."

Seth just looked at Marcus for a moment, but Marcus just looked back. Pointedly, he opened the letter, shook out the pages with flair, and began reading. Seth grumbled as he got up and filled a plate. He sat back down and began eating. At one point, he glanced at Marcus and blinked in surprise.

His little brother's facial expressions seemed to be running the gamut of emotions. Anger, surprise, humor, and confusion flickered across his fine features in rapid succession as he flipped through the pages. When he finished reading, his face registered regret. His gray eyes roamed around the kitchen, and Seth could almost see his mind working.

"Marcus? What is it?" Seth asked.

Marcus jammed the letter in his pants pocket. "None of your business, big brother!" he said. He turned and walked out of the kitchen, slamming the door behind him.

Seth was so shocked that he just stared at the door until Dean came into the kitchen. "What in tarnation was that?"

"Marcus."

"What did you do to him?"

Seth shook his head and went back to eating. "I don't think it was me. He got a letter from Claire."

Dean laughed. "Oh, is that all?"

"I don't know, Dean. He was really funny about it. Then he yelled at me and called me 'big brother.'"

"Well, you are his big brother," Dean said.

"I'm aware of that, but he doesn't ever call me that. Something weird happened, Dean. Mark my words," Seth stated.

Dean sighed. "I'll see if I can get it out of him later on."

He eyed Marcus's coat that was still hanging on a chair. After a moment of hesitation, he picked it up and put it on. It was incredibly soft and heavy. It was no wonder Marcus didn't get cold when he wore it. "How does it look on me?"

Seth considered him for a minute and then said, "Like you got swallowed up by a wolf. You can't pull it off. On him, it's perfect, but you? Nah. Sorry."

Dean took it off and realized that if Marcus's coat was there, it meant that Marcus was riding home with no coat. He shook the coat at Seth.

"I think you're right, Seth. Something is definitely wrong."

CHAPTER 4

*D*ear Marcus,

      I would like to thank you for proving my point that all men are chauvinistic. You and others have recently bolstered my opinion about this subject. In the male mind, all the female sex is good for is bearing children and keeping a house. When women attempt to improve their lives and become more than just property, they are knocked down or made fun of for being ambitious.

      It's obvious from your last remarks that you do not think I have what it takes to finish my degree or that you think I am too flighty to do so. It's also apparent that you think I am lazy and worthless because I do not have employment. I find this particularly offensive because if it were up to me, I would indeed find work. As it is, I am trapped and I can understand why Tessa ran away. She wanted to live her life on her own terms, and she has done that. I envy her and Maddie greatly.

      Men have been like this ever since time began and it seems that your sex has not evolved very much from the Neanderthals! You have no idea what it's like to be a woman. To be told what you can and cannot do. That your dreams and hopes are meaningless and unat-

tainable! Do you know what that does to a person? No, because you've always been able to do as you wish.

Mark my words; I will graduate and, for your information, I'll graduate with honors. Can you say that? No. How does that make you feel? Knowing your sharp intellect and thirst for knowledge as I do, I can imagine it does not feel good for you to know that you are not able to attend college. Take that and multiply it by a thousand and you might come close to what I feel.

I do not care to comment on the Mendel studies or anything else at this time and may never want to again. What is the point of learning when I can't put any of it to use? I won't be bothering you anymore.

Goodbye Marcus.

Claire

Marcus put the letter down. He still couldn't figure out what had happened. For three years, he and Claire had exchanged letters and, while they'd argued, they'd never had such a disagreement. Something had happened to incite this kind of rage, and he didn't believe that all of it was directed at him.

He read the letter one more time. Claire said she would like to get a job, but couldn't. It must have something to do with Geoffrey. Marcus knew that women of Claire's station were not expected to work. It wasn't considered good form for women to do any other work except helping with charities and domestic pursuits. He plopped his feet up on his kitchen table and pondered how to answer her.

After giving it much consideration, he picked up his tablet and pencil and began to write.

Dear Claire,

I'm not going to beat around the bush. I know that we harass each other about a lot of things and that we're always trying to best each other, but your last letter confused me and made me angry. I don't think my comments to you were any worse than anything you've ever said to me, so I fail to understand from where all this animosity is coming.

We've been writing each other long enough that I can read between the lines. Something else must be fueling the fury contained in that letter, and I think I deserve to know what it is. I know our relationship has been contentious from the beginning, but believe it or not, I'm actually a good guy and I get along with almost everybody. I'm willing to lend an ear, so to speak.

So if you want to write back and tell me what's going on, I'll listen. If not, that's your choice.

Marcus

P.S. I take offense to being lumped in with all the men who think that women are possessions or only good for breeding. Women out here are valued for the work they do and aren't held back from doing very much. As you know, in our way of life, the men are sometimes gone for long periods of time and the women have to be self-sufficient. I just wanted to be clear about that.

CLAIRE PLACED Marcus's letter down on her desk and rested her head on her forearms. The morning after she'd written that horrible letter to Marcus, she'd regretted it. She'd gone to retrieve it from the mail basket on the table in the foyer, but the mail had already been collected for the day.

She'd fretted about it for a week and a half until his reply had come. She felt terrible that she'd taken things out on Marcus when they had nothing to do with him.

"I should have waited to answer him until I was calmer," she mumbled into her arm. She needed to apologize to Marcus, but she didn't know how to begin. Perhaps a walk in the garden would clear her head and help her figure out what to say.

It was cold out and the early April breeze was brisk. She wrapped her cloak tightly around herself as she strolled along the paths. The wind blew into her face, making her think about Marcus outside with their cattle during the frigid nights. She wondered how he kept warm. She smiled as she pictured him with his dark hair that he wore a little long and his mesmerizing gray eyes.

Claire had been struck by his dark, handsome looks and captivating smile the moment she'd first met him. However, she could tell that although he was pleasant to her, he did not feel the same way about her. When she'd overheard him say something to Seth about Maddie's "kid sister," it had stung to know that he thought of her as a child. That was when her antagonism toward him had begun.

He'd been working out in the barn the day after she and her parents had arrived for Maddie's wedding. She'd gone out to see the horses, and he was in the haymow. Claire had watched him climb part of the way down and then jump the rest of the way. His landing had been easy, his movements fluid and graceful.

Marcus had turned and been startled at the sight of her. Then he'd laughed, and the sound was rich and warm. He had the kind of laugh that made people want to laugh along even if they didn't know what he was laughing about.

"Morning, Miss Claire," he said. "I didn't know you were there. Did you sleep well?"

She nodded. "Yes. Very well, thank you."

Claire had always been awkward around attractive men, and Marcus was even more intimidating because he seemed a little more primal than the men she knew. He didn't have Seth's bulk and he wasn't quite as tall as Dean, but he was a little broader in the shoulders than Dean was. Claire told herself that her careful study of his physique was purely scientific in nature. The womanly part of herself called her a liar.

Marcus had taken off his hat and shaken hay from it. He also brushed some off his shoulders. Without his hat on, Claire could see his gray eyes better and thought them the most beautiful eyes she'd ever seen. His smile flashed, and she'd been further entranced.

"Good. Glad to hear it. Hey!" he suddenly shouted. He leaped past her and swatted at Nugget, who had been going after Claire's hair.

Claire had jumped, and Marcus had seen her movement. He took hold of her upper arms and moved her to the left, away from the stall in front of which she'd been standing. She could feel the warmth of his hands through her dress. They were strong yet gentle.

"Sorry, but Nugget here has a special liking for hair. You'll have to watch yourself around him," Marcus said, scowling at the draft horse. "He's not mean, just playful. He's strong, though, and would hurt you without meaning to."

He released Claire and stepped away, and Claire had felt as if the sun had gone behind a cloud.

"So do you like to ride? We've got some good horses you could use," he asked.

"No. Yes," Claire said. She was flustered and couldn't get the words out right. "I mean, I like to ride, but I'm not very good at it. I do like to pet the horses, however."

Marcus nodded. "Well, we can't all be good at everything. Lord knows I'm not."

Something wet and furry touched Claire's hand, and she squealed and jumped, banging into Marcus's hard chest.

"Hey, whoa," he said once more, grasping her arms. "It's just my dog, Roscoe, saying hello. Sorry about that." He laughed and said, "You're having a rough start to the day. You shoulda seen your face. Sorry, but it was funny."

Claire had felt like he was making fun of her and struggled out of his grasp. "Release me. I'm not another pet to be mauled," she said.

Marcus had pulled his hands back from her in a gesture of surrender. He clearly hadn't expected that kind of response from her. "I'm sorry. I never thought you were a pet, and sure wasn't trying to maul you."

"I'm glad you find this amusing. You have unruly animals. You should train them better," Claire chided him.

Marcus's left eyebrow had arched. "They're trained well. Any animal can be mischievous and all Roscoe did was sniff your hand, something dogs are well known to do."

Claire had felt her temper ignite. "Do not condescend to me, Mr. Samuels."

"Then don't get your nose all bent out of shape over nothing," Marcus retorted.

"You have very bad manners," she told him.

"Me? You're the one insulting my training methods and expecting animals to behave perfectly," Marcus countered. "That's highly unreasonable."

"Is there a problem here?"

Seth had come unnoticed into the barn. He'd heard loud voices outside and wondered what was happening.

Claire smiled at him and said, "Nothing I can't handle, but I think I will go play with Mikey. He's much better company." She strode off without another word to Marcus. As she'd walked away, Claire had heard Seth berating Marcus.

AS SHE REMEMBERED the rest of that visit, she realized what a thorn in the side she had been to Marcus; while he'd argued many points of science and literature with her, he'd never been cruel. When his temper became too hot, he would simply walk away from her. That had happened at Maddie and Seth's wedding reception. They'd been debating all kinds of things and she'd pushed him too far.

He'd thrown up his hands and walked outside to cool down. She'd followed, and Marcus had turned to her with a fierce expression and said, "Claire, I've put up with all I'm going to put up with tonight and I'd appreciate it if you would allow me to enjoy the rest of the reception. Can you do that?"

Claire had recognized that he was barely holding his tongue in check and that it was time to leave well enough alone. "Yes, of course. I've been thoughtless. My apologies."

She'd gone back to the party and made sure to avoid him. The next day, however, they were back at it again. And so it had gone until they'd left.

Claire thought about his last letter and realized it must be true when everyone in Dawson said that Marcus was good-natured and caring. Even though she'd been rambling angrily in her letter, he'd exhibited kindness and had extended an offer of help. She debated whether to write him back, but couldn't make up her mind.

CHAPTER 5

arcus was once again playing short-order cook for his family. He'd just fed Mikey when Tessa walked into the kitchen. She walked up to him and wrapped her arms around him. Dean and Seth exchanged glances, and Seth shrugged his shoulders.

"Thank you, Marcus. You are my savior," Tessa said as she hugged him close. "Whatever is in that tea you make for me works wonders and has gotten me through that awful morning sickness period." She released him and kissed his cheek.

Dean thought he saw Marcus blush. "You're welcome, Tessa. Glad I could help."

"Not only that, you took over my cooking duties. I'm not sure how I'll ever repay you," she said.

"I do. You make me one of your peach cobblers and we'll call it even," Marcus said. "I want it all to myself, too."

"Done," Tessa agreed.

Maddie came into the kitchen and said, "Marcus, will you please make me some scrambled eggs?"

He laughed. "I think I need to open a restaurant. Of course I will."

After he'd served her a plate of fluffy scrambled eggs and toast in front of her, he set about mixing up another concoction of some sort. Dean made a face as the scent filled the kitchen. "Good God, Marcus, what is that one?"

Marcus didn't answer. He poured it into a cup and placed it in front of Maddie. "Let that cool a little and drink it."

She sniffed it and wrinkled her nose. "I don't think so, Marcus."

He gave her a level stare. "If you want a baby, drink it."

Maddie stared at him for a moment and then picked up the cup and blew on it until it was cool enough for her to sip. She made faces as she drank, but downed every drop.

"Good girl. I'll make that for you for the next three days and that oughta do the trick as long as you and Seth do your part every day. Understand?" Marcus said. "Every day."

Seth and Maddie looked at each other. A big smile came to Seth's face. "I think we can do that."

Maddie blushed and laughed. "Yes, I think we can."

LATER IN THE MONTH, Maddie and Seth left for Pittsburgh. Tessa was very disappointed that she couldn't go to Claire's graduation with them, but she sent a present along for her, as everyone except Marcus did. As Dean began to drive away with her sister and brother-in-law, Tessa's eyes welled with tears. She felt an arm settle around her shoulders and looked up at Marcus.

He reached down, rubbed her growing belly, and said, "If ever there was a good reason to have to stay home, this is it. You're taking good care of my niece."

Tessa laughed. "So you think it's a girl?"

"I do. Call it a hunch," he said as he caressed her stomach.

Tessa didn't take any offense at Marcus's hands-on approach. That was just the way he connected with people. He wasn't afraid to wear his heart on his sleeve. Normally, you never had to guess where you stood with him. He kissed her forehead and left her.

He spotted Mikey running through the paddock and sprinted in his direction. After jumping the fence, he grabbed Mikey and threw him in the air. Mikey let out a loud laugh, and Marcus threw him again and again until he was out of breath. Then he put him down and sent him off to Tessa, who'd watched the whole thing and laughed with them. Marcus was always able to cheer her up. Because of that, she hated to dampen his good mood.

Tessa walked over to the paddock. "Marcus, I need to tell you something."

Marcus ambled over and waited for her to speak.

"When Maddie and Seth come back, Claire is coming with them," she said, watching his face.

Marcus gave her an odd look. "Why?"

"To visit of course, silly," she said.

Marcus looked up at the sky and then down at the ground before looking into her dark blue eyes. "Has she said anything to you about me?"

"No, I'm afraid not. Should she have?" Tessa asked.

He pursed his lips and shrugged. "I haven't heard from her recently, but I don't know why."

Tessa laughed. "Don't tell me you've begun to enjoy her letters."

"Heck, no! It's just that I don't want her telling Seth I've done something wrong and getting me in trouble. He's completely blind to your sister's more negative attributes," Marcus protested, covering his true feelings.

Tessa nodded. "Oh, yes. I'm well aware of Claire's penchant for arguing and being an all-around pest. Try growing up with her."

"I'm glad I dodged that bullet. Well, I'd best get to fixing that broken stall door. I want to have it done before your husband gets back."

"I'll leave you to it, then," Tessa said.

As he headed to the barn, Marcus saw Jack riding up the lane and waved the boy down. "Come with me to the barn. I want to talk to you about something."

"What about?" Jack said as he dismounted.

Marcus smiled. "Let's go into the barn. It's private."

CHAPTER 6

*C*laire was nervous as she walked across the stage to receive her diploma. She was not always graceful, so she walked slowly and carefully. If she tripped or fell, she would be mortified. As she accepted the diploma from the president of Pennsylvania College for Women, she turned and saw her family several rows back.

All of them were smiling, and Maureen and Maddie were dabbing at their eyes. Seth gave her one of the winks that he reserved just for her, and she smiled back at him. However, she missed Tessa and Dean and wished that Marcus could have been there to see it. *That would have shown him,* she thought.

Claire sat down and felt pride in herself that she had graduated earlier than some of the students with whom she'd started her college career. She'd worked hard on a few subjects, but most of it had come easily to her. Dejection stole over her the next moment when she realized that she had earned a teaching degree that she might never put to good use.

Seth saw the look on her face and wondered what had caused it. Claire had seemed so happy before the ceremony, and she should be proud of herself. He certainly was, and so was the rest of her family. Then she brightened again and seemed fine.

Geoffrey and Maureen threw a huge party for Claire, and it was a very joyous event. Seth did his best to keep her laughing by dancing with her and teasing her about the handsome young men who danced with her. Claire had a good time, but she kept picturing a dark-haired man with gray eyes and wishing he were there.

It was a mild night toward the end of May, and Marcus was whittling on his porch. A lantern provided light so he could work on the piece of wood. It was almost done, and he intended to finish it that night. He turned the piece of wood this way and that, examining it critically. It was a small model of an apple with a worm coming out of a hole in the fruit. He'd put a smiling face on the worm.

The apple and worm sat atop a small book that said "Teacher" on the spine. With his small tools, Marcus had created the look of pages on the other side of the book. He hoped Claire would like it. She, Maddie, and Seth were due to be back the next day. He was just getting ready to paint it with the expensive paints that Tessa had bought him for his birthday when he heard a familiar hoot owl call.

He grinned. "Come, brother," he said in Lakota.

Black Fox, one of the braves from the nearby Lakota tribe, leaped up onto the porch and dropped down in the chair next to him. He was a very tall, powerful Indian with obsidian eyes and a slightly sharp nose. Since it was such a warm night, he was only wearing his loincloth.

"Hello, brother," he said to Marcus in English. "How are things?"

"Fine, and you?" Marcus asked. He'd spent a lot of time with the tribe and had taught some of them quite a bit of English.

"Fine. I bring news and a present," Black Fox said. He noticed Marcus's project and held out a hand. He was always interested in seeing what Marcus was working on.

Marcus handed him the present for Claire, and Black Fox

inspected it closely. The brave handed it back and asked, "What does it mean?"

"It's a present for my sister-in-law's sister. She just graduated college, and I wanted to make something special for her. This word says 'teacher.' *Waunspewichakhiye* in Indian."

"I see," Black Fox said with a laugh. "Is it for this Claire woman that keeps sending you letters?"

"It is."

"If you are bothered by her letters so much, why do you make her something nice like this?"

"Because it's expected of me and my oldest brother will kill me if I don't give her something."

"Are you sure that's the only reason?" Black Fox teased.

Marcus gave him an annoyed look. "Yes. So what's this present?"

Black Fox let out a call, and another brave stepped into the light. Marcus recognized He Who Runs. He was carrying a large bundle.

"Welcome, brother," Marcus said.

"Thank you, brother," He Who Runs replied. "We did not see you much over the winter."

Marcus switched back to Lakota. "I know. It was a hard winter and there was a lot of work to do around the ranch."

Black Fox snorted. "Your White family works too hard. They should try to have more fun like us."

Marcus gave him a hard stare. "How many times have I told you that I do not want you badmouthing my family? Now what the heck did you bring me?" he asked, gesturing toward the bundle He Who Runs carried.

He Who Runs came up on the porch then and handed it to Marcus. It felt solid and warm. Then it moved, and Marcus almost dropped it in surprise. Black Fox laughed and quickly reached out his hands to keep it from falling. The blanket fell away, revealing a baby. Marcus gave both Indians startled looks.

"What's going on?" he asked in English.

"Marcus, Silver Ghost, Samuels, meet your daughter, Aiyana,"

Black Fox said.

"*What?*" Marcus yelled.

The baby jerked in surprise.

"Is this a joke? If it is, it's a really bad one, Black Fox," Marcus said. "She's not mine."

"Oh, but she is. You remember One Bird's daughter?" He Who Runs asked.

Marcus smiled. "Yeah. She's not someone you forget," he said, thinking of Redtail, the beautiful Indian girl he'd spent so much time with the year before.

"This baby is hers. Or was." Black Fox's face became a picture of grief. "She was killed in a Cheyenne raid last week."

Marcus blinked at him a few times as he absorbed that information, then his eyes filled with tears of grief. Redtail had been a sweet, loving young woman, and Marcus had planned to see her again. Her loss moved him deeply.

He swallowed and said, "I'm so sorry, for the tribe and myself. Will you please tell her father that my heart is full of sorrow for him and the rest of her family?" He didn't speak her name because the Lakota didn't say the names of their dead aloud for fear that their spirits would remain earthbound.

He Who Runs nodded.

"How do you know she's mine?" Marcus said, looking at the baby.

Black Fox smiled. "Look at her eyes." He tipped the lantern a little so the light shone on the baby's face.

Marcus sucked in a breath as he recognized his own gray eyes staring back at him. "Okay, she's mine, but what am I going to do with her?"

He Who Runs laughed. "Raise her, stupid."

"What about One Bird or Aiyana's aunts? Wouldn't she be better with them?"

Black Fox shook his head sadly. "They already have their hands full with the children they now have. She is best with you, Silver Ghost."

He Who Runs placed another bundle on the porch.

"Please don't tell me that's another baby," Marcus said in a pleading tone.

Both men laughed at him. "No," He Who Runs said. "These are supplies for her. There is milk in here and mush. She is around eight moons old and can have a little in her milk. There are also cloths and moss." The latter were what the Lakota used as diapers.

"That will get you through until you can get some more," Black Fox said, rising from his chair.

"Wait. You're really going to leave her here with me?" Marcus said. His chest began to constrict with panic.

"Yes, brother," Black Fox said. "She's yours and belongs with her father now that her mother has gone to the Big Sky."

"You don't understand," Marcus protested, shifting the baby to his shoulder. "My White family doesn't know anything about all of you, remember? They won't understand. Please help me."

He Who Runs looked at Marcus with sympathy. "Silver Ghost, if your family is as wonderful as you say, they will get used to the idea of having Aiyana in the family."

His half brothers left the porch and disappeared back into the night. Marcus looked at his daughter, who smiled at him. He saw Redtail in her, but he couldn't deny that Aiyana looked like him, too. He returned the adorable baby's smile. She reached out and grabbed his nose, and he laughed.

He gently dislodged her chubby little fingers from his nose and said, "That'll be enough of that, little one. That's no way to treat your *niyate*," he told her, using the Lakota word for father.

She laughed, and Marcus fell in love with her as her silver eyes met his. "Yes, Aiyana, I'm your father," he said.

He sat holding her and playing with her until she rubbed her eyes as she became sleepy. Marcus didn't know where he was going to put her to sleep that would be safe. He had no crib or cradle.

"The wood box," he whispered.

He would have to clean it out, so he had Roscoe follow him into the house and laid Aiyana on his bed. Then he propped the pillow up on one side of her and rolled the blanket up and put it on the other side. Sarah and Tessa had both done that kind of thing with his niece and nephews. Then he told Roscoe to lie down and watch her.

The wood box was about the size and shape of a cradle and would do until he could get set up better. As he cleaned it out, Marcus tried to figure out how he was going to tell his family about Aiyana. Would they reject her because of her Lakota heritage? He decided that if they did, then they might as well reject him too. They didn't know it, but he didn't get all of his looks from his mother. He had her eyes, but his black hair and slightly darker skin belonged to the Indian who'd sired him.

Marcus dreaded how they would look at him once they knew. He'd known since he was sixteen but hadn't been able to tell them. When their mother had passed away, Marcus had gone through her things, just looking at them and remembering moments from his childhood. He'd opened the drawer of her nightstand and noticed a stack of journals.

He'd never seen them before and he began reading them immediately. When he was halfway through the fourth book, he had come across information that knocked the foundation out from under what he'd believed about his identity. His father had been away on a cattle drive when his mother had been attacked by a Lakota brave who was out for a good time. He'd forced himself on her and she'd become pregnant with Marcus as a result.

Marcus finished cleaning out the wood box and went back inside with it. He got another blanket and put it in the box, then laid Aiyana on the blanket. She was still sleeping peacefully. Marcus thought of Redtail and began to cry. He sat down on the sofa by his daughter and mourned the baby's mother.

He looked at the baby and said, "Aiyana. Eternal blossom. You sure are as pretty as any flower. Oh, little girl, how am I going to explain you to your uncles, aunts, and cousins?"

Marcus wiped away his tears and lay down on the sofa. He dangled a hand down so he was touching the blanket. All through the night, he lay awake, keeping watch over his daughter.

CHAPTER 7

*T*essa wondered where Marcus was. He was supposed to have been there already. There was work that needed doing, and Dean hadn't been pleased that his brother hadn't shown up that morning. Tessa and Sadie had cooked breakfast and then begun the laundry. Tessa wanted to have it done by the time her family returned.

Out on the road, Dean and company were having a good time catching up and talking about Claire's graduation. Maddie was telling stories about when Claire was little, and Claire was laughing even as she tried to make Maddie shut up. As they passed by Charlie and Lydia's place, Dean spotted something moving in the distance. When it got a little closer, he recognized Marcus's horse.

Marcus was riding flat out, but he checked Rosie's speed a little and turned her toward the pasture fence. Seth saw him, too, and he grabbed the reins from Dean and pulled the team to a halt.

Dean would have called out, but Seth clapped a hand over his mouth. "Shut up, Dean. You'll startle them and make them crash into the fence. They don't know we're here."

Dean nodded, and Seth dropped his hand. They watched Rosie bunch her haunch muscles and launch herself up and over the barbed-wire fence with grace and power. As she landed, they heard Marcus let out a war whoop and saw him pat Rosie on the neck.

"Well, I never," Seth exclaimed. "That's how he keeps coming down through the south pasture to the paddock. I suspected, but I didn't know for sure."

"That reckless idiot," Dean said. His tone was filled with reproach.

"Yep. But you gotta admit it was kind of pretty," Seth said.

Dean looked up at his brother. "What's the matter with you? Don't you realize what would have happened if she hadn't cleared that fence? She'd be permanently injured or dead. The same goes for Marcus."

"I know, I know. We'll have to talk to him about it," Seth agreed.

Claire had watched the jump with fascination and dread. Her hands had balled into fists as she mentally tried to help the mare over the fence. She didn't want to see either of them hurt. When they landed safely, she released the breath she'd been holding and sagged with relief.

Maddie took her hand. "I feel the same way. I can't believe he did that."

Claire nodded but inside she felt admiration for Marcus's bravery, even though it had been a reckless stunt. Her heartbeat was still elevated slightly as they turned into the lane to the ranch. When they arrived at the house, Marcus was waiting there with Tessa. He stepped forward and helped Maddie down, then reached up for Claire.

She paused for a moment before stepping forward. He took her around the waist and she put her arms on his strong shoulders. He lifted her down and set her on her feet. She was surprised to see him smiling at her as if he was happy to see her.

"Hi, Claire," he said.

"Hello, Marcus," she replied. She'd been anxious the whole way there because she didn't know what kind of greeting she would get from him.

Then Tessa was hugging her and exclaiming about how grown up she looked. Marcus assessed Claire and privately agreed. She'd blossomed as a woman, filling out in all the right places. Her hair caught the sunlight and Marcus noticed gold and red highlights. He hadn't seen that the first time she'd been there, but then again, he hadn't been looking at her in that light. He'd mainly been trying to keep away from her.

She looked at him shyly and then away again, and Marcus thought that he saw her blush a little. He blinked and then smiled. Then Dean stepped in front of him and said, "We have something to discuss, Marcus."

"Okay, sure. Uh, later, okay?" Marcus said. He grabbed a couple of bags from the wagon bed. "Are these yours?" he asked Claire.

"Yes," Claire answered.

"I assume Claire is in the guest room?" he asked Maddie.

"You assume correctly," Maddie replied.

Marcus nodded and walked over to the house. Claire walked with him and said, "Please be careful with them. I have a few things in there that are a little fragile."

"Okay. I need you to do me a favor," he said.

Claire looked at him. "Me? What could you possibly want *me* to do?"

"We'll take these to your room and then you pretend to start an argument with me and then I'll leave like I'm mad and you follow me to the barn," Marcus said in one breath.

"Why would I do that?"

"Because you owe me. That last letter you wrote was really nasty even though I'd done nothing to provoke your anger. Then you never even answered me. You could at least do me this small favor. I need to talk to you about something. Please, Claire?"

Claire thought about it for a moment, then said, "What's in it for me?"

"Whatever you want," Marcus growled. "I'll make it worth your while."

"All right," Claire said. Her curiosity got the better of her and she just had to know what he wanted to tell her.

"Thank you."

They entered her room, and Marcus set the suitcases down and stood back.

"What shall we argue about?" Claire asked.

Marcus rolled his eyes. "Do I have to think of everything?"

Claire crossed her arms over her chest and the movement emphasized just how much she had filled out. Marcus also noticed the gold flecks in her brown eyes for the first time. She had very pretty eyes. "This is your plan, Marcus."

He sighed. "How about the whole Mendel thing? We never did finish discussing that subject."

Claire nodded. "Yes. That will work because I happen to think you're wrong that you can alter the genetic makeup of peas."

"You're kidding, right?" Marcus said, raising his voice.

Claire followed suit. "No, I'm not. As a matter of fact, your notion is ridiculous."

Marcus began walking out of the room. "Listen, lady, take it from someone who grows plants for a living, you can definitely alter it. It's called a hybrid, or maybe you hadn't heard of that, Miss College Graduate," he yelled over his shoulder as he stomped through Maddie and Seth's parlor.

"Don't take that tone with me, Marcus Samuels," Claire said. They were down the porch steps and into the driveway by this point.

Marcus turned and bowed to her. "And what tone would milady like me to take?" he asked, and then walked away from her again.

Seth and Maddie stood on the porch and watched them disappear into the barn.

"Not even here ten minutes and they're at it," Seth said.

Maddie laughed. "I know. They're entertaining, to say the least."

Then they went inside and started to unpack.

MARCUS HAD Claire stay just inside the door while he ran all through the barn to make sure no one else was in it. He was slightly out of breath when he came back to her. He smelled of sweat, hay, and horse. Claire liked the combination.

"Let's go in here," Marcus said, indicating the tack room. He shut the door behind them.

"Now what is it that you want to discuss?" she asked.

Marcus started pacing. "I need your help, very badly. Outside of myself, you're the smartest person I know and I need you to put that brain of yours to use."

Claire frowned. "Very well. I'll try, depending on what it is."

"You have to swear that you won't tell a soul. Not until I'm ready to tell them myself. Do you swear?" Marcus pleaded.

Claire was starting to become alarmed. Marcus was clearly quite upset.

"Do you swear, Claire? I don't have a lot of time here," Marcus insisted.

"Yes. I swear. Now tell me what it is," Claire said.

Marcus raked a hand through his hair and then said, "I have a daughter, Claire."

Claire stared blankly at him a moment and then said, "I'm sorry, but I thought you said that you have a daughter."

"I did. I have a daughter. She's part Lakota Indian. She's adorable. Her name is Aiyana, and she's eight months old. I just found out about her when my half brothers brought her to me last night. A brave from my tribe, uh, forced himself on my mother and she got pregnant with me. Seth and Dean, don't know anything about my Indian heritage or the fact that I have a whole other family. They're not going to want me anymore when they find out, Claire. I don't know how to tell them, but I have to because I have this little baby now and I have to care for her and I need help to do that. I need you to help me figure out how to tell them. I don't want to lose them."

Claire leaned back on a saddle rack that was hanging from chains attached to the ceiling. It moved, and she almost fell. Marcus caught her with cat-like speed and righted her.

"Careful," he said.

She was trying to absorb everything he'd just told her. She closely examined his face and could now see his Indian heritage in his high cheekbones, black hair, and tanned skin. Something told her it was like that all over his body and she quickly squelched that thought. Her agile mind quickly sorted through the information Marcus had provided and she sought possible solutions.

Claire had come to Montana with an agenda of her own, and she now saw a way that she and Marcus could help each other.

"I'll help you. I think I have an idea, but I need your help, too."

"With what?"

"I want to stay in Montana, but my parents aren't going to allow it. I just know they won't." Claire dropped her eyes as she screwed up her courage, then looked him in the face again. "But they would have to if I were to marry someone who lived here."

Marcus gave her a confused look. "You want me to help you find someone to marry? Okay, sure, no problem."

"I've already found the person," she said. "You."

"Me?" he almost shouted. "Me?"

"Yes, you, dummy. I'm not talking to anyone else, am I?" Claire rolled her eyes. "You need someone to help you raise this child and run interference with your family for you. I can do both of those things. And I need to stay here and have a life of my own. I love my parents. They're wonderful people and very dear to me, but I'm a grown woman and can make my own decisions. Please, Marcus?"

Marcus thought over his options and realized that he didn't have much of a choice. "Do you really think we can get along? I mean, all we do is fight."

"We're not fighting right now," Claire pointed out.

Marcus smiled. "No, we're not, are we? Very well. It's a deal. We gotta make this look good, though."

Footfalls sounded on the barn floor outside the door. Claire quickly grabbed Marcus and pressed her mouth to his.

"What are you doing?" Marcus mumbled against her lips.

"Making it look good, dummy," she mumbled back. "Now kiss me."

Marcus did a mental shrug and wrapped his arms around her waist. He was surprised to find that she felt good in his arms. Claire put her arms around his neck. She'd only ever been kissed once in her lifetime, and that hadn't gone especially well. As a result, her technique was a little awkward.

"Claire," Marcus said. "Just hold still. I'll do the rest until you get the hang of it."

Gently he tipped her head where he wanted it. If the situation hadn't been so serious, he would have found their predicament laughable. He wished he had a little more time to teach Claire how to kiss, but he hoped that she'd learn fast.

Claire was embarrassed that he could tell that she was inexperienced. She willed her mind to clear and to just follow his lead. His lips were warm and supple, and Claire thought of how many times she'd dreamed of kissing him like this. His shoulders were firm under her arms and she instinctively placed her fingers on the back of his neck and ran them through his hair.

It was so soft and silky and she enjoyed playing with it. Marcus was surprised to feel his body break out in gooseflesh as her fingers grazed his skin. She smelled good, but he couldn't quite place the scent. His arms tightened around her and he ran his hands up her back. Her mouth was soft and pliant under his, and he felt her start to respond to what he was doing.

Thatta, girl, he thought. *Keep it up.* Claire was truly getting caught up in what they were doing and she kept wishing that it would go on forever. Her fingers tangled in Marcus's hair and she pulled a little. Marcus growled his pleasure against her mouth, and she pulled harder.

Sweet Jesus! Something snapped inside Marcus and he forgot that they were supposed to be playacting. He backed her up against the wall and ran his hands down her sides and back up. Then the door to the tack room opened, and a man cleared his throat. He had to clear it again before Marcus heeded it. Reluctantly, he pulled his mouth from Claire's and turned to see Dean standing in the doorway.

43

Marcus gave him a sheepish smile and Claire looked down bashfully. Marcus was acting, but Claire was not.

"You mind telling me what's going on here?" Dean demanded. His face was red with anger and his eyes were slits of blue fire.

Marcus's Adam's apple bobbed, and he looked back at Claire for a moment. "Uh, well, what does it look like?"

Dean stepped forward quickly, grabbed Marcus's neck, and marched him from the tack room. "Don't you smart off to me, you stupid idiot."

"Dean, I can explain," Marcus said as he turned around and backpedaled.

Dean kept coming, pushing him away from Claire, who had followed them. "I'm sorry about this, Claire. Get up to the house, Marcus. We've got a lot to sort out."

"Listen, Dean, you don't understand," Marcus tried again.

"Too right, I don't. Move it, Marcus," Dean said with a last push that landed Marcus on his rear in the drive.

Dean couldn't remember ever being so furious with Marcus. He grabbed the back of Marcus's shirt and began hauling him up. Marcus had finally had enough, and his own anger flashed. He got hold of Dean's hand and twisted his wrist. Dean cried out and released Marcus's shirt.

Marcus jumped up and faced off against his brother. His gray eyes were stormy with rage. Claire had never seen anyone fight before and she stood back watching in fascination.

"Leave me alone, Dean. I don't want to hurt you," Marcus said.

Dean laughed. "Hurt me? I think you got that backward."

"I'm tired of you bossing me around. I'm twenty-nine years old. Too old for you to push around anymore," Marcus shouted.

"Then start acting like an adult," Dean yelled back.

Tessa and Jack came out of the house to see what was happening. They were quickly followed by Seth and Maddie.

"You act like you're God's gift to this place and you know better than anyone else what needs doing, even though I've been doing it my whole life!" Marcus said.

"Someone has to keep you in line and keep this place running while Seth is away on drives and you're goofing around," Dean said.

Marcus laughed. "Yeah. Goofing around by being out on the coldest nights of the year because you can't hack it? Seth I can understand, but you?"

Tessa stepped forward as if to break things up, but Seth motioned to her to stay put "Leave them be. This has been coming for years. I have no idea what started it, but it needs doing," he said.

"*I* can't hack it? Who do you think used to do it before you were old enough?" Dean said.

"Well, I guess you're starting to feel your age then, huh? Getting older now, Dean," Marcus taunted him.

"I'll show you who's old," Dean said and came at Marcus.

Dean swung and Marcus ducked and rammed into Dean's midsection, landing them both on the ground. Dean slammed a fist on Marcus's spine, making him grunt in pain. He rolled away and jumped up. Dean gained his feet and Marcus began fighting Indian style. He'd spent many hours wrestling with his Lakota brothers and it was second nature to him now.

He dropped down and swept Dean's feet out from underneath him. Dean crashed to the ground and Marcus got ahold of him and wrapped him up in a move that left their audience standing with their mouths open. Seth had never seen anything like it, and he had no idea where Marcus had learned it.

Dean struggled but couldn't get loose. Marcus squeezed Dean's midsection tighter with his legs, constricting his breathing until his lungs couldn't expand enough to get a full breath. Dean began feeling lightheaded and his struggling grew weaker from lack of oxygen. Marcus waited until he knew Dean was on the verge of passing out and then released him and kicked him away from him.

Marcus's breathing was ragged and his voice raspy as he said, "You ever come at me like that again or take ahold of me like I'm some kid and I'll do a lot worse to you than that. That's a promise, Dean."

The group on the porch had a hard time reconciling this Marcus with the affable, fun-loving man they all knew and loved. His black hair was wild and his eyes blazed. His stance was defiant, as though he was daring anyone else to take him on.

When he saw the shocked expressions on their faces, he suddenly smiled. "He'll be fine, folks. His head might hurt a little and his ribs might be bruised, but other than that, he'll be good as new in a couple of days."

Marcus walked over to Claire with a huge smile on his face. "Pucker up, darlin'," he said. Then he cupped the back of her neck and kissed her soundly before going to the paddock and slipping through the fence. He caught Rosie and mounted her. Leaning down, he undid the gate and passed through. Then he closed it and was off in a trail of dust.

Seth ran to Dean, got him up off the ground, and dusted him off a little. "You okay, Dean?"

Dean swayed as dizziness enveloped him. "What the heck just happened?" he asked, shaking his head to try to clear his foggy brain.

Seth laughed. "Little brother just kicked your backside, that's what."

"What was it that he did? That thing with his legs?" Dean asked as Seth got under his arm and started leading him toward the house.

"I don't know, but I'd sure like to know how to do it. He did it slick as a whistle. I didn't know he could move like that," Seth said.

Tessa rushed out to meet them. "Dean! Are you all right?"

"Yeah. I think so. I'll be okay. Just give me a few minutes," Dean reassured her, although he felt it might take him more than a few minutes. "Stop! Seth, stop!"

Seth halted, and Dean threw up right on Seth's boots.

CHAPTER 8

*C*laire was sitting on Dean and Tessa's sofa, being grilled by the rest of her family.

"Claire, I'm afraid I don't understand what's happening between you and Marcus," Tessa said. "Would you please explain it to us?"

Claire cleared her throat and looked at the floor for a few moments.

Seth leaned over and put a hand on her knee. "Claire, you and Marcus have always hated each other, so we're confused why Dean found you, um, doing that."

"Yes, I can understand why you are surprised," Claire said.

"I'd say we're more than surprised, Claire," Dean said. He was sitting in his chair with a cold compress on his forehead. His head pounded and his ribcage hurt when he moved.

Seth grinned at the funny picture he made. Tessa glared at him, and his smile quickly faded.

"All right. Shocked then," Claire amended. "I think 'hate' is a strong word. We've disliked each other. At least it started out that way. I'm not exactly sure when, but our relationship began to change. We still argued about many things, but it was less antagonistic."

Claire found that her lies came easily because there was some truth behind them. She raised her eyes and looked at each of her sisters in turn. "The two of you know that one can be attracted to someone through letters. Is it really such a surprise that it would be the same for Marcus and me?"

Tessa thought back to the letters she and Dean had exchanged. Although Marcus had actually written them, she'd come to understand that the sentiments in them had been Dean's. She had indeed been attracted to Dean and had badly wanted to meet him and his children. Running away had been the best thing she'd ever done, and she was thankful that she'd had the courage to follow her dreams.

Seth and Maddie exchanged loving glances and held hands. Their letters had been of a slightly different nature. At Tessa's request, Seth had reached out to Maddie in her time of need and drawn her out of the deep depression she'd fallen into after her terrible ordeal at the hands of Theo Wilson. Theo had been a close childhood friend who had turned vicious when Maddie had spurned his romantic advances.

Remembering something more, Maddie smiled at her husband and said, "I've never thanked you for what you did the night before you left to come back here."

"And what was that?" Seth said.

"Don't play dumb, Seth. I know it was you who took matters into hand and exacted your own kind of justice on Theo," Maddie said.

Tessa looked at Seth, and Dean even took the cloth off his forehead so he could see his brother.

"Is that true, Seth?" Tessa asked.

Seth looked uncomfortable as he said, "Yeah. It was me. I just couldn't leave without making sure he knew what it felt like to have that happen to him."

Maddie hugged him and said, "Thank you. You don't know how much it meant to us. In many ways, it was a better punishment than any court could have handed down."

Seth kissed her cheek. "You're welcome."

Tessa turned back to Claire. "So you're telling us that you and Marcus fell in love through your letters to each other?"

"I think that 'love' is also too strong a word," she hedged. "However, we are quite enamored of each other. One reason I came back to Dawson was so we could spend more time with each other and see where things might lead."

Tessa could imagine why someone would fall in love with Marcus. He was engaging, likable, and handsome. He also had a knack for making people smile and he was wonderful with children. Dean always said that it was because he was still a kid himself. Dean had found out earlier that Marcus was no kid, though.

Tessa hated to admit it, but she sometimes thought that Dean was harder on his younger brother than was necessary. Even so, she didn't want to interfere. Dean was kind and considerate to others, but he seemed to feel the need to be strict with Marcus. He was much the same way with Sadie, and it was causing a rift between Dean and his daughter. Tessa knew it was over Tucker Foster, the boy Sadie had started courting.

Dean was afraid that Sadie was going to get her heart broken and kept saying that she was too young to be courting. Tessa tried to remind Dean that Sadie was almost seventeen and was becoming her own person. She also pointed out that he and his first wife had been the same age when they'd started courting.

Claire thought it was time for her to begin conducting her part of the bargain she and Marcus had made. She only hoped that he would live up to his as she sat up a little straighter and said, "Now, I have something to say to all of you. There are some things that Marcus needs to discuss with you that are of the utmost importance. He was going to do this today, but things happened that prevented him from doing so." She gave Dean a pointed look that held strong disapproval.

Dean held her gaze for a second and then dropped his eyes.

"Now, when he tells you his news, I beg of you to keep an open mind and remember that he is still the person you all know and love," she said, looking at each of them in turn. "You are all so important to him and he deserves your respect and understanding. It is not my place to tell you this news, but I feel that he will not be angry with me for saying this much. I've said all I'm going to say, so please don't ask me any questions."

She rose and left the room. They heard the kitchen door open and close. The four of them exchanged puzzled looks and wondered what Marcus had to tell them.

～

CLAIRE WALKED to the paddock gate on shaky legs and leaned against the fence for support. She took deep breaths to steady herself. She'd never told so many lies. Whether they were half honest or not, they were still lies. She felt guilty, but also felt the ends justified the means. The deception was necessary in order for them to be able to achieve their goals.

She put her head on a forearm and thought about Dean and Marcus's fight. She laughed over the fact that it had enthralled her to see something so violent. Claire admitted that she had been proud that Marcus had come out the victor. When Seth had helped Dean up, she had covered her mouth, not out of shock, but because she had to stifle the laughter that had bubbled up inside her.

Her smile faded as she remembered Marcus's kiss before he rode away. That had been exciting, but in a different way. The possessive way that he handled her had been thrilling, and she hadn't minded in the least.

Suddenly, Seth was beside her. He draped his forearms over the fence and looked down at her. "So, you want to tell me what's really going on with you and Marcus?"

"What do you mean? I've already told you," Claire said.

Seth nodded. "I think you've told some of it, but I'm good at reading people and I can tell that there's more to the story."

Claire looked down. She should have known that Seth would see through her. Still, she wouldn't betray Marcus's confidence. Neither would she lie to Seth.

"I can't say any more than I already have. I made a promise to

Marcus and I'm going to keep it. You'll know when the time is right, and that time is up to him," Claire explained.

Seth sighed. "You know, a lot of people don't know how crazy secrets drive me. Pa used to say that I was too curious for my own good. He was right, but I can't help it. So this is *really* making me nuts. I hope he doesn't wait too long." He laughed. "How about the way he took care of Dean?"

Claire looked at him in surprise. "It surprises me that you find it humorous."

"I'm not the only one. I saw you laughing," he said, nudging her with his elbow.

Claire laughed. "Yes. I'm afraid I did find it funny. I couldn't help myself."

"It's okay. I'm not mad about it. I love Marcus, but I'll tell you right now, you've got your hands full with him. Dean's half right about him. He has a tendency to start something and then not finish it. That really ticks Dean off. Dean is a little too serious about some things, but he means well. Pa always told us that we were going to have to make Marcus toe the line to get him to do the things that needed doing. I guess Dean took that to heart a little more than he should have. He can be a pain in the neck, but Marcus is the most fun person I know and can make you laugh even if you don't want to. He's always been like that."

"I can see that about him now. I didn't before, but I do after today."

"When he was little, he got away with all kinds of stuff that Dean and I couldn't. He was so sweet and used it to get out of work or to keep from getting yelled at. He's good at talking in circles, too, and makes you forget what you were talking about. And pranks? He's pulled some good ones on everyone, including me," Seth told her.

Claire smiled as she imagined the antics of the three brothers growing up. "If it's as you say, it looks like I'm in for quite an adventure."

Seth gazed out across the pasture to the steers that were grazing peacefully there. "I have a feeling that we all are."

CHAPTER 9

*B*lack Fox heard Marcus's familiar hoot owl call and smiled. His half-breed brother was back within the time frame he'd promised. He made the sound of a warbler to let Marcus know where he was and waited. Suddenly Marcus appeared, and Black Fox wondered again how Marcus walked soundlessly in cowboy boots. That ability and his silver eyes had earned him the Lakota name "Silver Ghost."

Black Fox frowned as he looked at Marcus. "Looks like you've been tussling with someone," he commented.

Marcus smiled. "Yeah, my brother Dean."

"Were you practicing wrestling?"

Marcus laughed. "Something like that. Where's my *michunwintku*?"

"Your daughter is with Wind Spirit," Black Fox said. "She has been enjoying her."

Wind Spirit was Black Fox's wife.

Marcus said. "Thanks for watching her. I really appreciate it."

"Did you speak to your sister-in-law's sister?" Black Fox asked as they walked toward the Lakota camp.

A lopsided smile appeared on Marcus's face. "I sure did."

Black Fox recognized that smile and put an arm around Marcus's neck, shaking him a little. "I knew it. You *do* like her."

"I wouldn't go that far," Marcus said seriously. "You know, my brother Seth and you would get along. You're a lot alike."

Black Fox gave him a doubtful look.

"No, it's true. You both like to tease the heck out of me and you're about the same size. Well, you're a little thinner than he is, but other than that," Marcus insisted.

"That's because I don't eat as much as you say he does," Black Fox said with a laugh.

"I don't know about that. You just eat different things."

Black Fox nodded. "True, but I do like that peach stuff your sister-in-law makes."

"Peach cobbler," Marcus said. "Say it: peach cobbler."

"Peach cobbler," Black Fox said. He'd found the English that Marcus had taught him over the years useful. He also enjoyed learning new skills.

Marcus smiled. "You got it. Good job."

When they reached the camp, of the children who came running to them.

"Uncle!" one boy said. "I have missed you!"

"Raven, I have missed you, too. Are you well?" Marcus said to his nephew in Lakota.

Black Fox's son nodded. "Yes. Come see the carving I made." The little fellow took Marcus's hand and led him to Black Fox and Wind Spirit's tipi. He disappeared inside and was back in seconds.

Marcus took the piece of wood Raven handed him. The boy had made a small horse. For an eight-year-old boy, it was a fairly accurate depiction. Marcus couldn't resist sitting down so he could examine it closer. He crossed his legs and turned it this way and that, using the sunlight to study it.

"Raven, this is excellent work," he said.

Raven's bright smile flashed and his dark eyes held pride.

"Do you want to know how to make it even better so you can give it to a pretty girl one day?" Marcus said.

Raven laughed. "Yes, Uncle."

Marcus got caught up in instructing his nephew on how to improve the carving. He didn't do the work for him, but he showed Raven what needed to be done. Raven watched with rapt attention, nodding his head and asking questions. When Marcus finished, the shadows were growing long.

He rose as Wind Spirit came walking into the clearing. She'd been out on one of the trails, collecting berries and bark. Aiyana was strapped to her back in the ornate cradleboard that He Who Runs had made for her.

Wind Spirit smiled as soon as she saw Marcus. Marcus hugged her and kissed her cheek.

"You get more beautiful every day," he told her in Lakota.

"So you say. You are such a flirt," she told him, her dark eyes smiling up at him. She took off the cradleboard and handed it to Marcus. "Here is your daughter. She has been a joy."

Marcus took Aiyana from her and looked at his daughter. She smiled and reached for him, and his heart was filled with love for her.

Black Fox said, "You look good with a child, Silver Ghost."

"Thanks," Marcus said.

Wind Spirit went into the tipi and came back out holding a large bundle. "Here are more cloths and moss. It will keep you supplied for a few days."

"What do you think your White family will say about Aiyana?" Black Fox asked.

Marcus kissed his daughter and then shrugged. "I'm about to find out."

Black Fox nodded. "Good luck, brother."

Wind Spirit echoed his words.

"Thanks," Marcus said.

As Marcus walked the trail back to where he'd left Rosie, his apprehension grew. His stomach hurt and he felt a headache coming on. What he was about to do could cost him his first family and he didn't know how he would handle that should it come to pass. He didn't have a choice, though. His daughter had to come first.

Although Marcus liked to have a lot of fun, he always carried out his responsibilities. He'd already become dedicated to the little baby strapped to his back, and he loved her with all his heart. He lashed the bundle Wind Spirit had given him behind his saddle and mounted Rosie carefully. Keeping the pace to a trot so Aiyana wouldn't be bounced around too much, he set out for the ranch. Along the way, he stopped at his house and then rode on. As he rode, he prayed that Claire had kept her promise to him and had paved the way for him to tell his family about Aiyana and his other life.

AS NIGHT BEGAN TO FALL, Claire paced back and forth in front of the barn. She didn't know where Marcus had gone and had no way to find out. Going to his house was out of the question because she didn't know where he lived and didn't feel confident riding there alone. It had been a long time since she had ridden a horse and she might fall off. Nor did being alone in the woods at night appeal to her.

She couldn't stay still, however, and kept moving to work off some of the nervous energy that filled her. Dean was sitting on the front porch, watching her. It seemed like she was waiting on Marcus and he wondered what she knew that they didn't. Seth and her sisters had tried to get her to tell them, but she wouldn't give up anything. Had Marcus told her he'd be back tonight or was she just worried? He didn't know, but it didn't sit well with him that Marcus had some kind of secret.

Dean rubbed a hand across his ribs. They ached, and he wondered if Marcus had cracked a rib or two. Tessa had examined him, and they'd found that there was some light bruising across his torso. Dean felt angry and ashamed at the same time. Angry that Marcus had bested him and ashamed at the way he'd treated Marcus. He deserved what Marcus had meted out, and he knew he would have to change his attitude toward his brother some. If anyone had pushed him around like that, Dean knew he would have struck back.

Claire turned toward the drive as if she'd heard something, and Dean leaned forward. Tessa came out of the house and stood by him. Claire thought she'd heard a horse's hooves on the dusty lane. A lone horse came trotting into view, and she recognized Rosie, even in the moonlight. The horse's white mane gave her away.

Marcus pulled Rosie to a stop in front of Claire. He looked down at her with a question in his eyes, and she nodded up at him. "I've done everything I could. Is that her?" she asked, pointing to the cradleboard on Marcus's back.

"Yeah. Wait 'til you see her," he said grinning. "She's a beauty."

Claire smiled. "I'm sure she is."

"C'mon. Might as well get it over with." He moved on, keeping Rosie at a walk so Claire could keep up. "I'm gonna keep my end of the bargain, Claire. I made you a promise and I won't go back on it."

Claire smiled. "Everyone was very surprised at the turn in our relationship, to say the least. It was somewhat amusing. Seth knows that something is odd about it, though."

"I'm not surprised," Marcus said. "He's pretty good at rooting out the truth. He has a sixth sense about stuff. Plus, he's nosy."

"Dean is feeling the effects of your fight," Claire said with a soft laugh.

Marcus smiled. "I'm not surprised. Serves him right."

Dean and Tessa stood up as they approached the porch. Marcus let out a high-pitched whistle, and Seth poked his head out of the door at the sound.

"Get your wife and come over here," Marcus called to him. "Let's go inside where there's light."

He dismounted slowly and waved all of them into the house ahead of him. Looking up at the night sky, he took a few cleansing breaths before entering the house.

"Marcus," Dean said.

Marcus held up his hand and said, "Dean, you can apologize later. I have something much more important to tell you."

Dean quieted and gave the floor to Marcus.

Marcus looked each of them in the eye and said, "I hope you will still want me in the family after I tell you everything. Don't forget how much I love you and that I'm still me."

Tessa and Dean exchanged curious glances as Marcus continued. "There's someone I'd like to introduce to you." He took the pack from his back and placed it against the kitchen door. Aiyana looked out at him from the cradleboard.

None of them could see around Marcus to see what he had. Marcus smiled at his daughter, then stood up and turned around. "Everyone, I'd like you to meet my daughter, Aiyana."

Total silence met his announcement, then Dean said, "Your *what*?" His voice was loud in the kitchen, and it startled Aiyana, who began crying.

Seth reached out a long arm and smacked Dean on the back of the head. "You scared her, you idiot. Keep your voice down." Then he looked at Marcus and said in a hushed voice, "Your *what*?"

Marcus didn't answer either of them. He comforted his daughter, speaking to her in a language the others had never heard. Tessa listened closely, but couldn't identify it. It certainly wasn't European. She and her sisters were well versed in French and Italian. This was a more guttural language, but beautiful in its own way.

They watched Marcus talk to the baby and blow raspberries on her little belly. She laughed and looked at them, and they saw her gray eyes that were so like Marcus's. The group knew then that he was telling the truth and not pulling some kind of prank on them. Dean looked at the cradleboard and then back at the baby. He'd seen cradleboards like that when he'd run across Indians. It all began to add up.

"Marcus, you have a daughter and she's part Indian?" he asked quietly.

Marcus said, "Yep. And so am I." His smile was filled with pride. "Isn't she beautiful?"

CHAPTER 10

Seth laughed. "Marcus, I know you have a good imagination, but you being part Indian is impossible. Both our parents were White. I believe that she's half Indian, but not you."

Marcus held Aiyana out to Claire. Claire didn't know anything about holding a baby, so she took her hesitantly. Patiently, Marcus showed her how to hold Aiyana and prevent her from falling. "There you go. I'll be right back." He ran out the door.

"You knew about this?" Tessa asked.

Claire nodded and looked into Aiyana's eyes. She was a beautiful baby and Claire could see Marcus in her. Aiyana reached out and grasped Claire's nose.

"Ow!" Claire said. She took Aiyana's hand from her nose and held it.

The baby wrapped her little fingers around Claire's forefinger as Marcus returned. He handed Seth a book and said, "This is one of Ma's journals. I found them after she passed away. I marked the page where you need to start reading."

"Marcus, what's this got to do with you?" Seth asked.

"Please, Seth. Just do as I ask."

Seth sat down, opened the journal, and took out the paper bookmark. As he read, his eyes got wider and at one point he made a fist and almost slammed it on the table. At the last second, he seemed to remember the baby and hit his leg instead so it didn't make much noise. Dean wondered at the black look on Seth's face. Then tears gathered in his brother's eyes and he wiped at them. When he had read all he could stand, Seth stood up and slapped the journal against Dean's chest. Dean took it, and Seth left the house.

Dean looked at Marcus, but the other man wasn't giving anything away. He started reading, looking up at Marcus every so often. The others guessed he must have come to the same passage that had caused Seth's anger because he sat down heavily in one of the chairs. Maddie and Tessa looked at each other, and then Maddie went after her husband.

Marcus took Aiyana back from Claire and Tessa watched him with her. He played with her the same way he'd played with Mikey when he'd been a baby. Dean finished reading and looked at his brother in a new light. He wasn't sure what to make of Marcus; now that he knew the truth, he could see his Indian features. Catherine Samuels had had dark brown hair, but not black. Marcus's eyes were hers, but his other coloring came from his biological father.

"You're my half brother?" Dean asked.

Marcus gave an apprehensive nod. Tessa looked shocked, but Marcus only had eyes for his brother at that moment. With a huge effort, Dean swallowed his anger.

"This Indian, your father–" Dean began.

"He's not my father, Dean," Marcus cut in. "Pa was my father. The other guy just happened to sire me, but he wasn't my pa. I want to be clear about that."

"Okay," Dean said, conceding the point. "The other guy who 'sired' you, is he still alive?"

"No. He was killed in a raid a few years after I was born," Marcus said.

"And how do you know this?" Dean asked.

"Because my brothers told me," Marcus explained.

Dean felt like someone had punched him in the chest and he

couldn't breathe for a moment. Tessa saw him go white and put a hand on his shoulder. "Do you want some water?" she asked.

"No, thanks. I'm okay," Dean said. "You have other brothers besides me and Seth?"

Marcus nodded. Aiyana reached for his nose, and he moved his head away from her. "Yeah. Three. And a sister. Two sisters-in-law and various nieces and nephews."

Jealousy and anger consumed Dean, and he wanted to hit something. "So she's really yours," he stated, pointing at Aiyana.

"She has a name, Dean. Aiyana," Marcus said.

Somehow, Dean kept a tight rein on his emotions. "Aiyana is yours. So are you married to an Indian woman?"

"No. Her mother was killed in a Cheyenne raid about a week ago," Marcus said. He closed his eyes in grief for a second.

Claire's breath caught in her throat and she felt sympathy for Marcus even as she felt jealousy for this other woman that Marcus had obviously cared for.

Marcus opened his eyes and looked at Dean again. "I know this is all so hard to understand or accept right now, Dean, but I hope you'll be able to someday. You'd like my other brothers. He Who Runs is a lot like you; fierce and serious."

Dean got up from the table and walked back and forth like a trapped cougar. He kept looking at Marcus and his baby and away again. Some things started clicking in his mind. The weird concoctions Marcus had started making for them, the easy, loose way that Marcus sat on a horse, and the moves he'd used that afternoon came back to him. He stopped and turned to Marcus again.

"So you've known since you were what? Sixteen? You were sixteen when Ma died, right?" Dean asked.

Marcus nodded.

"And you never thought to enlighten us about all of this?" Dean asked. A vein in his forehead throbbed and his headache grew worse.

Marcus sat down and bounced Aiyana on his knee. "Would you have if you'd been me? Think about it, Dean. My mother had just passed away. I was heartbroken. I was even younger when we lost

Pa, and her death only compounded my grief. Then I read that and discover that not only was our mother raped, but I'm the product of that assault, and half Indian to boot?"

Tessa laid a hand on Dean's arm. "Anyone would be terrified, Dean."

"Yeah, I was. I didn't have any parents left and I couldn't risk losing you and Seth, too. I wouldn't have had anyone in the world," Marcus said. "Please don't abandon me now."

Dean snorted. "What would it matter if I did? You have a whole other family. Do they know about me and Seth? About all of us?"

Marcus couldn't answer, but his silence told Dean all he needed to know. Uncontrollable rage filled him and he swept a pile of dishes and cups from the counter. Marcus turned and curled his body around Aiyana to protect her as dishes and several cups came their way. They bounced off his back and landed loudly on the floor.

"Get out, Marcus! Get out and don't ever darken my doorstep again! Get out!" Dean screamed at him.

Aiyana became scared at all the noise and began wailing. Marcus grabbed the cradleboard and ran out the door. He leaned it against the house and quickly put her in it, murmuring words of comfort to her in Lakota. Once he had her on his back, he mounted Rosie and began trotting down the lane, even though he wanted to gallop.

"Marcus! Wait!" Claire came running after him.

He slowed for a moment, letting her catch up. "Take me with you! Please?" she said.

"Why? Why do you still want anything to do with me?"

"I don't care what your heritage is. It doesn't change my opinion of you."

"And what would that be?"

"That you'll never be as smart as me, no matter how hard you try," Claire said with a smile.

Her answer caught Marcus off guard and despite the horrible scene in Dean and Tessa's house and how wretched he felt, it struck him as hilarious. He stopped Rosie completely because he didn't trust himself to guide the horse properly while laughing so hard.

"So you wanna ride away with a stupid Indian, huh?" he asked when his laughter subsided.

"Yes, I do," Claire said. She didn't want him to leave her behind. She would have been worried sick about him.

"Back up a second," he said.

When she did, Marcus dismounted and started taking off the cradleboard. "Turn around."

"Why?" she asked.

"Well, we can't ride double if I'm wearing the cradleboard. You're going to have to wear it. Unless you're going to ride in front," Marcus said.

Claire's eyes widened. "I'll wear the cradleboard." There was no way she wanted to guide Rosie carrying such precious cargo.

"Okay. Turn around," Marcus said.

She did, and he took her left arm and put it through the strap and then did the same with her other arm. The weight that settled on her shoulders wasn't overly heavy. Marcus came around to stand in front of her and adjusted the straps a little. "There. Looks good. Okay, now up you go. Foot in the stirrup, give a bounce, pull on the saddle horn. I'll push from behind."

Claire did as he'd instructed, but she let out a little squeal when she felt his hand firmly grasp her rear end and help her up and over. Marcus laughed softly.

"Slide to the back of the saddle, Claire. I have to sit in it."

"I'm aware of that. It's hard with a dress on," Claire groused.

"We'll have to get you some leggings then," Marcus said.

Claire was shocked. "Pants?"

"Yep," Marcus responded. He climbed into the saddle in front of her. "Put your arms around my waist."

Claire hesitated, but when she did, she could feel the firm muscles of his torso and his body heat through his shirt.

"Tighter, Claire. I don't want you two falling off."

She hugged him tighter and smiled to herself. He felt incredibly good. Satisfied, Marcus started out again.

He swung Rosie around to face the ranch and looked at the place where he'd grown up. Marcus's heart filled with intense sorrow as he remembered all the good times he'd had there and the pride he felt in knowing that he'd helped to build a successful ranch. He mourned the loss of the close-knit family he loved. Then he turned Rosie around again and started up the lane to the main road.

Claire felt horrible for Marcus and angrier with Dean than she'd ever been with anyone in her entire life. Her anger turned to fury when she felt Marcus begin to cry. She inched even closer to him, then rubbed his chest and pressed her face against his back in an effort to comfort him. She'd only ever seen one man cry before and that had been her father one night after they'd brought Maddie home from the hospital. Her wounds had been horrible and Geoffrey had been overcome with grief and worry.

Marcus's sobs were quiet but powerful, and Claire shook with each jerky movement. Tears of sympathy fell from her eyes and dampened his shirt. They'd been traveling on the main road for a while before Marcus turned left down the road that led to his house. His crying was spent by that time.

He sighed and patted her hands. "Thanks."

"You're welcome." A wild idea formed in her mind. "Marcus, take me to meet your other family."

Marcus sat up straighter at that. "No, Claire. You don't have to do that."

"I want to."

Marcus thought about it for a moment and decided to test her. "Well, I guess you should meet them if you're going to marry me."

Claire raised her head from his back. "You still want to marry me?"

"I told you I was going to keep my end of the bargain. You tried your best for me. It's not your fault that Dean wouldn't listen."

"But won't that be awkward?" Claire asked.

Marcus shook his head. "No. Just because I can't go to the ranch anymore doesn't mean that you can't. I'll teach you how to ride a horse or we'll get a buggy and I'll teach you how to drive it so you can go see everyone."

Claire frowned. "You would do that?"

"Yes," Marcus said. "They're still your family. Dean kicked me out, not you. And don't try to be a martyr or noble and think that you shouldn't see them just because I can't."

She could hear the sincerity in his voice. "Very well. Now take me to meet your other family."

"You're really sure?"

Claire pinched him.

"Hey! Knock it off! Okay, we'll go," Marcus said. "Don't be afraid of them. They're just like us except they wear less clothing. And they sit around a fire. And they live in tipis."

"I know all that. I'm not completely ignorant of Indians, Marcus," she snapped.

He smiled at her irritated tone. "There's the Claire I know."

"Do you miss her?"

Marcus was confused. "Who? The other Claire?"

"No, dummy. Aiyana's mother. Do you miss her?" Claire asked.

"Is 'dummy' going to be your pet name for me? Because that's what you keep calling me," Marcus said.

"Answer the question, Marcus."

Marcus could tell it was important to her and that she wasn't going to let go. "Yes. It's complicated, though. We spent a lot of, um, private time together and she was a lot of fun to be around. She was kind and generous. We were friends more than anything. I didn't see her all the time because her clan wintered pretty far south, so I only saw her in the summers."

Claire nodded to herself, unsure of how she felt about that. She decided to put the matter aside for the time being. "Where are we going?" she asked.

"To my family's camp. It's down this trail."

"But we're in the woods," she said.

"How very astute of you, darlin'."

She pinched him again.

He grabbed her hand and squeezed hard. "You do that again and

I'm going to make you get off and leave you to find your way home."

Claire looked around at the black night and said, "Please don't."

"You promise you'll behave?"

Fear of being alone in the dark forest overshadowed her annoyance with him. Plus, she knew he wasn't going to release his painful grip on her hands if she didn't agree. "Yes."

He let go of her hand, and they rode in silence for a while. Claire felt Rosie tip forward as they headed down a steeper part of the trail. She hung on to Marcus tighter, and he grunted.

"Lean back a little," he said, pushing her with his own body, forcing her to do what he wanted. "We have to help Rosie keep her balance."

Claire shifted her weight back slightly even though she was terrified of falling off. Before long, the trail leveled out again and they shifted upright again. Marcus stopped and Claire felt him draw in a breath. A hoot owl sounded close by and it took her a moment to realize that Marcus had made the sound. There was an answer in the form of a nighthawk's cry. Claire jumped at the sound and Marcus squeezed her thigh and said, "It's okay. It's just my brother, Owl."

"His name is Owl?"

"Yeah. He's on sentry tonight. What did you expect his name to be, Bob or Tom?"

"No," she barely restrained herself from pinching him again. "Do you have an Indian name?"

"Yep. Silver Ghost."

Claire thought that sounded very romantic. "I like that. Why is that your name?" she asked as they started moving again.

"Because of my eye color and the fact that I'm very good at moving silently."

"Oh." Claire noticed that the trail was getting brighter and raised her head and tried to look around his shoulder. "I can't see anything."

"You will in about a minute," Marcus explained.

True to his word, they rode out into a huge clearing a few moments later. Tall tipis dotted the land, and numerous fires burned in front of them. Claire had never seen an Indian before and felt afraid as she looked around. All she knew was what she'd read about them in books.

Marcus hadn't been kidding when he'd said they didn't wear as many clothes. Most of the men were wearing loincloths that left much of their bodies bare. The women were wearing dresses that reached only about mid-thigh. Everyone she saw looked fierce and wild. She tried not to show it, but they scared the bejesus out of her. What had she been thinking when she'd insisted that Marcus bring her here?

Black Fox appeared beside Rosie, and Claire jumped a little. Marcus laughed. "Relax, Claire. This is Black Fox. He's one of my other brothers. Hello, brother."

Claire was shocked when Black Fox spoke in English. "Hello, brother. Is this the woman you've been writing to?"

Claire looked into Black Fox's face and saw humor dancing in his eyes. "You know who I am?"

"Yes. You are Claire. Writer of annoying letters," Black Fox said with a laugh.

"Claire, you can let go of me now. Black Fox, can you help her down?" Marcus asked. "She's not very experienced with riding horses and her legs are probably stiff by now."

Claire loosened her arms from around Marcus's waist and shrank back a little from Black Fox. The Indian noticed her movement but patiently held out his hands. Claire looked into his night-black eyes and something in them made her trust him. She leaned forward, put her hands on his shoulders, and let him lift her from the horse.

When he set her down, Claire's legs threatened to buckle. Black Fox hung on until she felt steady. "Thank you."

"You're welcome," Black Fox said. In Lakota, he said to Marcus, "Your White woman is pretty. With her brown hair and long legs, she reminds me of a fawn. That should be her Indian name."

Marcus climbed down from Rosie. "Okay, but let's ask her if she likes it." To Claire, he said, "Black Fox says you look like a pretty fawn and that Fawn should be your Indian name."

Claire smiled. "Really?"

"I think she likes it," Black Fox said in English. "Fawn it is. Now you must say it in Lakota, pretty Fawn. *Thingleska*."

Claire tried it and got it fairly well on the second try.

Black Fox was impressed. "She is smart, like you said."

Claire looked at Marcus. "You told him I'm smart?"

Marcus shot his big brother an annoyed look. "Great. Now she's not going to let me forget it."

Claire gave him a whack on the stomach, and Black Fox laughed harder. "Fawn has spirit, too. I like her."

"Thank you," Claire said. "You're not so bad yourself."

Black Fox's brow furrowed, and he looked at Marcus who translated. "I see. Thank you."

Marcus lifted Aiyana from the cradleboard and handed her to Black Fox, who took her easily. He was used to handling children. Then Marcus helped Claire get the cradleboard off her back. She hadn't realized it, but her shoulders were aching and she rolled them to loosen the knots in them.

"You'll get used to the weight and build up your muscles so it'll be easier to carry," Marcus assured her.

Claire didn't answer because several children ran up to encircle Marcus. They talked excitedly to him and pointed at Claire. Marcus knelt down and spoke to them. She heard her Indian name and could only assume that he was telling them who she was. She smiled at them. They were so sweet and of different ages, she noted.

She watched Marcus with them and saw how at ease he was with children. Suddenly, they all attacked him and he went down under a pile of small brown arms and legs. His rich laughter rang out and mingled with theirs.

Claire laughed as Marcus tried to get up and the group of eight children pulled him back down. Black Fox smiled; he could see why Marcus would be attracted to her, even if he didn't want to admit that he was.

"It is always like this," he told Claire. "He is good with them. A favorite uncle."

"I can see why," Claire said. "Here, I'll take Aiyana."

Black Fox handed the baby to Claire and watched as she shifted her to her hip. "You look good with a baby."

Claire was pleased. "Thank you."

Another Indian came up to them and spoke to Black Fox and gestured at Claire. This Indian was shorter than Black Fox and seemed a little more serious. Black Fox answered and then turned to Claire.

"This is He Who Runs."

Claire remembered the name Marcus had said at Dean and Tessa's. "You're Marcus's other brother."

"Yes. And you are Claire, the letter writer," He Who Runs said in English.

A flicker of annoyance passed over Claire's face, and Black Fox laughed. "I don't think she likes that name. She likes Fawn better."

"Yes, I do," Claire agreed.

Aiyana grabbed a handful of her hair and yanked it. "Ow!" Claire exclaimed, and the baby laughed.

Claire extracted her hair from Aiyana's grip and kissed her tiny hand. "You are so precious."

When Marcus was finally allowed to get up, he was breathless from tussling with eight kids. "Thanks," he said in response to her remark.

"Not you, dummy. The baby."

"There you go with 'dummy' again." He frowned.

He Who Runs chuckled and said, "I think 'dummy' is good."

Marcus glared at Claire. "Thanks."

She gave him a sugar-sweet smile. "You're welcome, Silver Ghost."

He Who Runs turned serious and switched to Lakota and asked, "So did you talk to your other family?"

Claire saw Marcus's face go from smiling to incredibly sad in an instant. He shook his head and walked off. Both braves looked at Claire for an explanation.

CHAPTER 11

*C*laire stared after Marcus until he disappeared from view, then looked at his brothers. Their expressions were fierce, and she swallowed in sudden apprehension. "Um, it didn't go well," she said. "He's very upset about it."

He Who Runs just snorted and followed Marcus.

Claire looked up at Black Fox and said, "I'm so sorry."

"It is what we expected. It is a shame. They are lucky to have him," Black Fox said.

"I know," Claire said.

"You love him," Black Fox said.

Claire couldn't believe that Black Fox could read her so well after just meeting her, but he was right. The truth was that she'd been in love with Marcus since they'd met three years before. There was no use denying it to Black Fox. She hesitantly looked at him as she nodded.

"But you are too scared to tell him," Black Fox said.

"Yes. Please don't say anything to him." Her voice was only a whisper.

Black Fox looked into her eyes and wondered why he should feel a kinship with this White woman who had irritated Marcus for so long. "It is not for me to tell. It is your secret."

She smiled at him in relief. "Thank you."

Black Fox motioned for her to follow him. He stopped in front of a tipi and spoke to a woman there. To Claire, he said, "This is my wife, Wind Spirit."

"Hello, Wind Spirit," Claire said.

The other woman was beautiful with long black hair and dark eyes. "Hello, Fawn," she said with a warm smile. "Come and sit. Would you like some tea?"

"I'd love some," Claire said, and then wondered where she was going to sit. There were no chairs.

Wind Spirit sensed her predicament. "Your dress is beautiful, but too long and will make it difficult for you to sit. Come with me."

Claire was curious as she followed Wind Spirit into the tipi. There were four sleeping pallets and various containers sitting around the edges of the tipi in an organized fashion. Different colored bags of all sizes made of deer and cowhides hung from the support poles. A hole in the top of the tipi would let out smoke when a fire was going inside.

Wind Spirit went over to a large basket woven from reeds and other materials. She opened it and pulled out some kind of garment. She brought it over to Claire and said, "Put this on. You will be more comfortable."

Claire looked at the dress and thought it beautiful. There was an intricate pattern of quills and beads across the front, and the bottom and sleeves were edged with tassels. When she reached out to touch it, she found it incredibly soft.

"I couldn't possibly take it. I don't want to take your clothes," Claire said.

Wind Spirit smiled. "I have plenty. My husband keeps me well supplied with hides. Please take it. It is rude to refuse a gift in our culture."

The last thing Claire wanted to do was offend Marcus's family. "Very well. Thank you."

Wind Spirit nodded, then took Aiyana from Claire and left the tipi. She closed the flap of skin that covered the doorway to give Claire privacy while she changed. Claire took off her dress and layers of petticoats. She stood in her bloomers for a while before she realized that she was going to have to take them off in order to put on the Indian dress.

Claire had never worn a dress that left so much of her skin bare. She was torn between propriety and fitting in with this people's culture. Finally, she decided on the latter and took everything off and quickly put on the Indian dress. It fit her well but left her feeling exposed. As she walked toward the door of the tipi, Claire had to admit that there was a kind of freedom in not being encumbered by so many clothes.

She took a breath and opened the flap and walked out. Marcus had returned and saw her emerge from the tipi. His breath caught as he watched her walk self-consciously toward the fire. He stared at her long, beautiful legs and her curvy hips and full bosom. She had taken her hair down, and it flowed over her shoulders. The firelight brought out the gold and red highlights that he'd seen earlier that day.

Claire looked at him shyly and waited to see what he would say. She watched his gaze roam over her body and she could almost feel it caress her. A fire ignited in his eyes and turned them silver in the firelight. He gave her a slightly lewd smile that told her he liked what he saw. She smiled back at him and then dropped her gaze.

Marcus came to her and said, "You are a *wikhoskalaka*. A beautiful young woman."

"Thank you," Claire said, knowing he could see her blush. She'd never had any man other than her father tell her she was beautiful. To have Marcus tell her that bolstered her confidence and made her feel womanly.

"Black Fox is right. You have pretty legs," Marcus said.

Claire's eyes widened, and she looked over at Black Fox, who shrugged and said, "It is true."

Marcus laughed at her surprise and took her hand. "Come with me."

Claire went willingly, enjoying having his hand wrapped around hers. "Where are we going?"

"I want to show you something."

"What is it?"

"Claire, shut up and wait," he said, but there was no bite to his words.

They walked along a trail that went down a gradual slope. Marcus guided her over branches and rocks, making sure she didn't trip. Claire couldn't figure out how he could see so well in the dark. All at once, the woods fell away, and they came out onto a huge rock ledge that looked over a river. The moonlight danced on the surface of the water that was moving in ripples as the current changed.

Claire realized how high up they were and grabbed onto Marcus as a wave of vertigo washed over her. Marcus said, "Claire, back away a little. It can be pretty overwhelming if you're not used to it."

She nodded and looked up at him. "Yes. I can see that."

He gazed out over the water and said, "This is my favorite place in the whole world. I come here to think a lot."

Claire felt honored that he would show her his special spot. "It's beautiful."

Marcus looked down at her, and she saw that fire in his eyes again. "Yes. Beautiful."

His arms came around her and his palms pulled her closer to him. His mouth curved up, and he asked, "You remember your kissing lesson from earlier today?"

Claire looked at his mouth and nodded.

"Good," he said. He dipped his head and brushed his mouth against hers.

Claire sighed, and Marcus captured her lips in a harder kiss. Her arms encircled his neck of their own accord and she gave herself up to him.

Marcus couldn't believe that this was the same Claire that had annoyed him so much over the past three years; the same woman who had never backed down from an argument and had challenged him at every turn. She was warm and willing, even in her innocence, and he wanted more.

Marcus ended the kiss but still held her close, his chest rising and falling. He couldn't remember a woman ever exciting him the way Claire did.

"What's wrong?" she asked.

"Nothing," he said. "That's the problem. We better head back."

"Why?" she said, looking into his eyes.

"Claire, um, let me put it this way; if we stay here kissing like that much longer..." he trailed off.

"Oh!" Claire said. She moved away from him a little. "I understand."

Marcus laughed and caught her face in his hands. "How is it that you've driven me crazy the past few years but I suddenly want you so much?"

"I don't know. I guess I'm just talented," she joked.

"Yes, you are. And the point goes to the lady," Marcus teased her, and then kissed her again. He decided to throw caution to the wind, as he often did. "You're opinionated, exasperating, too smart for your own good, and obstinate. That's how I used to see you and I still do, but I also now see that you're kind, beautiful, brave, and funny. I know this is not the ideal situation, but sometimes you just have to deal with things as they come. Claire I-don't-know-your-middle-name Fawn O'Connor, will you marry me?"

She didn't mean to, but she laughed.

Marcus simply looked at her. "Is that a yes or no?"

Claire couldn't talk at first, so she nodded vigorously. She found her voice and said, "I'm so sorry, but that must be the most touching and funny proposal that has ever been uttered in the history of the world."

Marcus then saw the humor in what he'd said and chuckled.

"I especially liked the 'I-don't-know-your-middle-name' part," Claire said.

"Yeah, that was kind of inspired, wasn't it?" he said.

He reached into his pocket. When he brought his hand back out, Claire saw something glimmer in the moonlight. She held her breath as Marcus took her left hand and slid a ring on her third finger.

"This was Ma's engagement ring. She left it to me with a note that told me to give it to a very special woman. You're that special woman, Claire."

In the moonlight, Claire could tell that it was an emerald instead of the traditional diamond. The setting was beautiful, and the craftsmanship was excellent.

"Marcus, it's extraordinary. I'll cherish it, and I'm honored that you would give me your mother's ring," she said.

He gave her a bashful half-smile and said, "I'm glad you like it."

She nodded, and he kissed her again. He would have released her quickly, but Claire didn't want him to stop and ran her hands up his hard chest, tracing her fingers along his ribs.

"That tickles," Marcus protested with a laugh. "Come on, fiancée, let's go back to camp."

CHAPTER 12

Seth came running when he heard a loud crash and screaming. He'd been out on the back porch of his house, thinking about what he'd just read. His long legs carried him rapidly around the house and across the drive. He stopped when he saw Marcus's horse trotting away. Shaking his head, he let him go and went into Dean and Tessa's place. He hadn't seen Claire running after his brother.

He stepped into the kitchen and almost slipped and fell as his booted feet came down on pieces of dishes. He skidded to a stop and looked around the room. Tessa was standing back against a wall, and Dean was by the stove amid more broken dishes and other kitchen items on the floor. The murderous gleam in his eyes told Seth that something very bad had happened.

"Tessa, you go on to bed. I'll take care of this," Seth said.

Tessa knew he was talking about Dean and not the mess. She threw Dean a look full of reproach and anger and left the kitchen. Seth heard the bedroom door shut and lock.

Seth had never seen Dean like this and wasn't quite sure what to expect. "Dean, what happened?" he asked softly.

Dean's jaw worked and his hands gripped the back of a kitchen chair. His knuckles turned white with the intense pressure with which he squeezed the wood. After several minutes, he raised his head, and Seth saw tears trickling down his face.

"He has kept all of this from us since he was sixteen. *Sixteen!* Thirteen years Marcus has known about what happened to our mother and that his... That *animal* raped her!" Dean said.

"I'm not happy about it either. I'm going to kill that monster," Seth said.

"You can't. He's dead. Marcus said he was killed a few years after he was born. Would you like to know how he knows this?" Dean asked.

Seth nodded. "I would."

"His brothers told him! His Indian brothers!" Dean practically screamed.

"Hey! Keep your voice down. Your kids are sleeping," Seth warned. Then he thought about what Dean had just said. "He has other brothers?"

Dean sneered at him. "Yeah. You left before he told us that. And get this; they know about us. They've known for years!"

That didn't sit well with Seth either. He couldn't believe that Marcus had been keeping so many secrets from them for so long.

"Oh, and he also has a sister and all kinds of nieces and nephews," Dean said. "And now a half-breed daughter."

Seth thought of the chubby little baby with Marcus's eyes and smiled. "You gotta admit that she's a sweet little thing. What's her name?"

"Aiyana, I think. That's not important right now," Dean said. "What are we gonna do?"

"I think we oughta find out some more about all this. I have a lot of questions, don't you?" Seth responded.

"I just can't," Dean said.

"Just can't what?" Seth asked.

"Deal with this. It's too much," Dean answered.

Something occurred to Seth. "Where's Claire?"

Dean's expression went blank for a moment. "I'm not sure. I

think she ran out after Marcus."

"Did she go with him?" Seth asked.

"I don't know!"

"What happened here?" Seth asked, pointing at the floor.

Dean looked around at the mess as if seeing it for the first time. "I lost it. All I remember is seeing red and telling Marcus to leave."

Seth made a sarcastic noise. "You didn't just tell him, you screamed at him. I heard you all the way out back of our house."

Exhaustion coursed through Dean and sapped his strength. He pulled out a chair and sat down. "Do you think Pa knew?"

Seth saw their mother's journal on the floor and said, "I don't know, but maybe the answer is in this." He bent and picked it up, then joined Dean at the table and opened the journal, making sure to flip past the place he'd stopped at. Leaning back in his chair, he settled in to read.

MARCUS AND CLAIRE rejoined the tribe. Claire noticed many of the people staring at her curiously and smiled at them. Some of them smiled back, but not all. She wondered what they all thought of her. They did greet Marcus, however. He stopped to talk to several of them and though Claire had no idea what he was discussing with them, she could tell that these people fully accepted him.

When they arrived back at Wind Spirit and Black Fox's tipi, they found Wind Spirit holding Aiyana. "She has been fed and changed," she said, handing her to Marcus.

"Thank you," Marcus said. "Are you ready for bed, little one?" he asked. Aiyana yawned as if in response.

Claire laughed. "I'd take that as a yes."

"Me, too. It's late. We'll just stay here tonight," Marcus said.

"We're going to stay here?" Claire said. "Where?"

"In my tipi," Marcus said.

Claire's shock showed plainly on her pretty face. "You have a tipi?"

"Quit repeating everything I say, Claire. Yes, I have a tipi. I stay here a lot."

"But what about your house?"

"I use that during the winter, but I'm here so much during the summer that I have my own tipi," he explained.

"Where?" Claire said, looking around. "Which one?"

"Follow me. Good night, Wind Spirit, Black Fox."

Claire bid them goodnight as well and then followed Marcus as he carried Aiyana toward their destination. Marcus's tipi wasn't too far from Black Fox's. It was smaller, though, and Claire surmised that it was probably because Marcus didn't have a wife or children. He wouldn't need so much space.

When they entered it, Claire looked around, curious to see how Marcus would decorate his tipi. She saw a lot of bags hanging from the support poles. "What is in all these? You have a lot more than Wind Spirit and Black Fox."

"Ah, Wind Spirit thinks of everything," Marcus said.

"What?" Claire said before she realized that he wasn't responding to her.

Marcus had seen a cradle that was already prepared. He kissed Aiyana and laid her in it. Then he stood up straight and stretched. Yawning, he began unbuttoning his shirt.

Claire watched as his tanned skin was revealed to her and felt her pulse rise. She decided to repeat her question. "What are all these bags?"

Marcus threw his shirt on the ground, not caring where it went. He yawned again and said, "Medicine, mainly. There's some tea and spices, but mostly medicine."

When he started undoing his pants, Claire said, "Marcus!"

Marcus stopped at her sharp tone. "What?"

She arched a brow at him, and he got her meaning. He gave her an annoyed look and unbuckled his belt and threw it next to his shirt. He kept the pants on, however. "You're gonna have to get used to it someday."

"Used to what?"

"My sleeping naked."

"What?" she said loudly.

His dark brows drew down. "Shh! Not so loud. You'll wake up Aiyana."

"I'm sorry," she said in hushed tones. "You sleep naked?"

Marcus nodded. "Yeah. I hate wearing clothes to bed. They just get all bunched up, and shirts strangle me." He sat on one of the two sleeping pallets on the floor and removed his boots and socks. "Oh, that's better."

"Your feet stink," Claire said.

"If you wore boots for as many hours a day as I do, your feet would stink, too," Marcus said in response to her critical tone.

He tossed the boots and socks out of the way.

"You're not very neat, are you?" Claire observed.

Marcus said, "Well, I've lived alone since I was eighteen, so I haven't had to worry about keeping my house spotless." He turned to look at her. "I guess that'll have to change."

Claire looked down at her beautiful ring. "I still can't believe you gave me your mother's ring and that you're still intent on marrying me."

Marcus lay down on his back. "Yep. Still intent on marrying you. That's what the ring is for."

"I know, but earlier today I was afraid you would change your mind," she said.

"Nope."

"About these bags?" Claire couldn't help her curiosity, and talking about something else would help distract her from the sight of his muscular torso.

"What about them?"

She found a small pebble and threw it at him. It bounced off his forehead. He laughed and rolled and pinned her down so fast it left her breathless. "What about them?"

"Um, uh," Claire fumbled as she looked into his eyes. "Why do you have them?"

"Can you keep a secret?"

She gave him an annoyed look. "I think I've already proven that I can."

"So you have," Marcus said. "I'm sort of a part-time doctor."

Claire drew back from him in surprise. "A doctor?"

"Or medicine man, if you will," he said. "*Waphiya.*"

"You're a doctor?"

"I think we've already established that. Not a traditional doctor, maybe, but a doctor nonetheless," Marcus said. "I became interested in medicine when I was younger and Doc Turner would come to treat us for some kind of ailment. He started teaching me and I really liked it. When I found out about my heritage and came here, I started learning from Wild Hare, the shaman at the time. I started blending White man's medicine with Lakota medicine, so it's kind of the best of both worlds."

"Do you treat our family?" Claire asked.

"Yeah. I helped Tessa get through her morning sickness with this baby. I made her an elixir that calms the stomach. I make them for headaches and poultices for wounds and all kinds of things," Marcus said. "I didn't start using any of it around them until a few years ago because I didn't want questions asked that I couldn't answer."

"That's amazing," Claire said.

Marcus shrugged. "It's something I wanted to do because I can't stand seeing people suffer. And because it keeps my brain sharp."

"It seems to be working. You seem to get through my books very quickly."

"Yeah, about that; nice of you to make fun of me because I can't go to college," he said.

Claire said, "I'm sorry, but sometimes you made me so angry with the things you'd say in your letters."

"Me? You started it all," Marcus said.

Claire started giggling. "I still remember that day in the barn when I got you in trouble with Seth."

He squeezed her bare knee, and she yelped because it tickled. "I could have killed you that day. He was so mad at me and I hadn't done anything wrong."

She laughed harder and Marcus said, "Shut up, Claire. Stop laughing at me."

It only made her laugh more and, eventually, he laughed along with her. "You sure have him wrapped around your finger. It's because you cut up his food all the time."

"Don't you make fun of me about that. Papa started it and I can't help it," Claire said, poking a finger into his chest.

"When we get married, will you cut up my food?" Marcus teased.

"Probably. So you might as well get used to it."

"I guess there's a lot we're going to have to get used to, huh?"

"I guess so," Claire agreed. "So let me see if I have this straight; you're half Indian, a doctor of sorts, a rancher, and incredibly smart? Does that about cover it?"

"Yeah, except the rancher part is now past tense," Marcus said.

Claire could have kicked herself for bringing that up. Gone was the laughing, teasing man, and in his place was a dejected man who'd been rejected by his family. "I'm so sorry," Claire said. "That was thoughtless of me."

Marcus sighed and gave her a sad smile. "It's okay. I have to face it at some point. Might as well start now. I do have to go back to the ranch, though. There are things there that are mine that I bought and paid for."

"Then you should have them," Claire said. She traced the line of his jaw with a finger. "They belong to you."

Marcus caught her hand and kissed her palm. She shivered and Marcus arched an eyebrow at her. "Are you cold?"

Claire shook her head a little. "No."

"Oh. So you don't need a blanket?" he asked.

"No." She reached up and hooked a hand around his neck and pulled him down to her.

Just then, Aiyana began crying. Marcus groaned and laid his head on Claire's chest. Claire felt his body start shaking with laughter.

CHAPTER 13

$\mathcal{A}$s dawn broke over the camp, Claire was still sleeping soundly. Aiyana was also sleeping. Marcus had been up for a little while, but he didn't want to wake them. He was sitting like an Indian, with his elbows resting on his knees, just watching Claire. He remembered when they'd first met and he'd considered her an annoying, spoiled brat.

She'd known how to push his buttons and did so at every turn. Marcus had been relieved when she and her parents had left. However, the peace had only lasted until she'd sent him that first letter. He'd known she was expecting a response, and he knew that she knew that if he didn't write back he was going to be in trouble with both families.

With a wry twist of his lips, he realized that she'd outsmarted him from the beginning. Through all the years they'd been writing, he'd kept picturing her as she had been then, not as the woman she'd become. Her smile captivated him and he liked making her laugh, something he didn't think she did enough. Originally, he had agreed to marry her out of desperation and because he'd promised her anything she wanted if she helped him.

Her idea about them getting married had taken him by surprise, but he'd known that she wouldn't have helped him unless he acquiesced. After they'd kissed in the tack room, he'd realized there was some attraction after all so it wouldn't be all bad if they did get married. He was grateful to her for trying to help him. Even if she hadn't completely succeeded, she'd given it her best shot.

Claire had outsmarted him again, it seemed. He knew she wanted to get married so she could stay in Montana, but it seemed like there was something else to it. She had him right where she wanted him. And it did seem that she wanted him, he thought, as scenes from the previous night flickered through his mind. He was going to have to watch himself around her.

Claire stirred. She'd been sleeping on her stomach, so she pulled her hair back from her face and rolled over. She looked around at her surroundings, trying to get her bearings, and jumped a little when she saw Marcus sitting on the ground.

"Hi, Claire," he said.

She gave him a sleepy smile and said, "Hi, dummy."

Marcus crossed his arms over his chest. "Is that any way to speak to your future husband?"

She didn't answer him. Instead, she crawled over to Aiyana's cradle and peeked in at the baby. Marcus watched with a smile, and he knew Claire would make a good mother to Aiyana. It seemed that she didn't mind either his or Aiyana's Lakota blood.

"Are you hungry?" he asked.

"Ravenous. What do you eat for breakfast here?"

"Bear stew," Marcus said.

Claire looked at him with wide eyes.

"Or deer stew, roasted buffalo, deer, or elk meat. Bread with berry sauce. Pretty much whatever you feel like or is left from the night before," Marcus said. "The Lakota are primarily a meat-eating people, but they do like potatoes and other vegetables. They also like Tessa's peach cobbler. It's Black Fox's favorite dish except for roasted buffalo. Sometimes in the winter, I give them one of my steers," Marcus said.

"You give them your cattle?" Claire asked.

"Sure. I stay here a lot, so I should contribute. I'm not going to let them starve, and they can always use the hides and other parts of the animal. There's very little waste."

"Yes, we studied about that in anthropology," Claire said. "It's fascinating getting to see it firsthand, though."

"I'm glad you appreciate it," Marcus said. "I only wish Dean and the rest would."

Claire crawled to him and kissed his cheek. "I'm so sorry."

"Me, too. But I don't want to think about that right now. Let's go eat," Marcus said, getting up.

Claire rose and looked at Aiyana. "Bring our daughter," Marcus said.

Startled, Claire could only stare at him.

Marcus shrugged. "You're going to be my wife and you said you'd help me raise her, right?"

"Yes," Claire said.

"Then you're her mother now, the same way Tessa is to Sadie and Jack," Marcus explained.

Claire looked down at Aiyana in a new light. Her daughter. She smiled as she picked the baby up and cradled her in her arms. Aiyana yawned, and Claire laughed. Aiyana didn't seem ready to wake up yet though and quickly settled back into slumber. Claire's stomach growled, and she quickly followed Marcus.

AFTER BREAKFAST, they thanked Marcus's family for the hospitality and left. Marcus felt it was time to show Claire his house and see what she thought about it. He didn't expect her to live in a tipi all the time; she needed to be introduced to that culture a little at a time. As they rode, Marcus started teaching her Lakota words by pointing to things and having her repeat their names.

She caught on quickly, as he'd known she would, and he made a game out of how much she could remember. He rattled off English words to see how fast she could come up with the Lakota name. They laughed when she fumbled around or mispronounced one.

When they came out of the woods into the clearing where his house stood, Marcus abruptly stopped speaking and pulled Rosie to a halt. There was smoke coming out of his stove chimney when there shouldn't have been. Cautiously, he moved Rosie forward at a slow walk until he could see around the front of the house.

Seth was sitting in one of the rocking chairs on the porch. His feet were propped up on the railing and his hat was slid down over his face. Trepidation bloomed in Marcus's breast as he wondered what Seth wanted. A grim determination came over him, and he rode Rosie up to the porch.

Seth tipped his hat back and smiled at Marcus. "There you are, little brother. Where've you been?"

Marcus smiled cautiously back. The fact that Seth had used his nickname was a good sign. "At my family's camp," he replied.

Seth nodded and said, "Hey, Claire. You doing okay?" He eyed her Indian dress with curiosity.

"Yes, Seth. I'm fine," she said. "Are you here to insult him or fight?"

A broad smile broke out on Seth's face. "No, Claire. Nothin' like that, I promise." He put his feet on the porch floor. "I made coffee if you want some."

Marcus dismounted and held up his hands to Claire, but she shook her head. "Let me get down on my own."

Marcus gave her a doubtful look. "You do remember that you have a baby strapped to your back, right?"

"Yes, dummy, I do," she said. She scooted forward and got herself onto the saddle. It was easier in her Indian dress. Then she put her foot in the stirrup, swung her other foot up over the horse, and slowly let herself down until her foot touched the ground. She slid her other foot out of the stirrup and smiled at Marcus.

"I did it!" she said excitedly.

"Yes you did," he said. He kissed her as a reward.

Seth's surprise at this affectionate gesture amused Marcus. Claire began taking off the cradleboard, and Marcus helped take it from her shoulders. Together they took Aiyana from the cradleboard. Marcus carried his daughter up onto the porch and looked at Seth. "What do you want?" he asked.

"Answers. I have a lot of questions and I think I deserve some answers, Marcus. Now, you and Claire go get some coffee and I'll hold my niece while you do that," he said. When Marcus didn't relinquish his hold on Aiyana, Seth said, "Marcus, when have you ever known me to harm a child?"

"Never."

"I'm not going to start now. Let me hold her."

"Marcus, Seth isn't going to hurt her. Let him hold his niece," Claire agreed before walking into the house. The scent of coffee wafted in the air and she couldn't resist it.

Marcus handed Aiyana to Seth and watched him smile at his niece. Seth looked her over and then sat her on his lap. "Darn, she's sweet, Marcus. She's definitely got your eyes. How old is she?"

"Eight months."

Aiyana spotted Seth's hat and reached for it. Seth let her have it and laughed as it fell over her head and face. He picked the hat up and started playing peekaboo with her. Aiyana laughed.

After a while, Seth put his hat off to the side and bounced her on his knee. "How long have you known about her?"

"Two days."

Seth gave him an incredulous look. "Two days? That's it?"

"Yeah. She's the only reason I told you and Dean all about me. I have a child to raise and I'm not going to hide her."

"I wouldn't want to hide her, either. Where's her mother?" Seth asked.

Marcus was getting tired of repeating himself about this. "Dead. She was killed in a raid about a week ago. That's why my brothers brought her to me."

Seth's lips pursed at the mention of Marcus's other family. "How many do you have?" He couldn't contain his curiosity, despite being jealous.

Marcus sat in one of the other chairs. It was apparent that Seth wanted his answers immediately. "I have three brothers and one sister. Black Fox is my oldest brother and he and his wife have a boy named Raven and a girl named Winona. He Who Runs is next oldest and is married to Eagle Woman. They also have a boy and a girl. Owl, who is only about a year older than me, is single and doesn't have any children."

Seth was fascinated. "Their names are interesting. Do you have an Indian name?"

Marcus nodded. "Silver Ghost."

"Why?"

"My gray eyes and because I can move silently when I want to," Marcus said.

Seth said, "Come to think of it, you do surprise me sometimes. I turn around and there you are and I never heard you come up behind me."

Marcus smiled.

"So that stuff you gave Maddie to drink? Was that a Lakota drink?"

"Yes."

Marcus jumped when Seth grabbed him in a one-armed bear hug. "It worked! Maddie's been sick in the mornings for about a week now and Dr. Turner just confirmed this morning that she's pregnant!"

Marcus's heart filled with joy. He hugged Seth back and slapped his back. "That's fantastic! Congratulations, Seth!"

Seth released him, but his grin remained. "We did what you said and did our homework every day."

Marcus laughed. "Good boy! Darn, I am so happy for you. But as great as that is, guess what?"

Seth frowned. "What?"

"I still beat you in the kid department."

"You're an idiot," Seth said with a laugh. "Don't worry, we'll catch up. Just keep making that stuff."

"It's called a potion," Marcus said.

"Okay. We'll go with that." That was Seth's standard response to something he didn't want to bother to learn.

Claire came out onto the porch and handed cups of coffee to the men then leaned down and kissed Seth's cheek. "I heard what you said. I am so happy for you and Maddie. I know how much you want children and have been disappointed it didn't happen before now."

"Thanks," Seth said. "Yeah, we were starting to think it wouldn't happen, but Marcus fixed that."

Marcus nodded. "I had to do something to help. I could have given it to her long ago, but I wasn't sure if I should because it might reveal my secrets."

"About that. How could you keep all this from us for so long?"

Marcus said, "Do you know about Dean's reaction last night?"

"Yeah."

"That's why. I've never seen him like that. He threw all those dishes and stuff all over the place. If I hadn't protected Aiyana, she could have been hurt. If that had happened, I would have killed him," Marcus said.

Seth saw the protective way Marcus looked at his baby and knew he meant every word he said. "After the way you handled him yesterday, I don't doubt you're capable."

Something fierce and wild flickered in Marcus's eyes, and Seth felt a prickle of fear along his scalp. "You have no idea how capable I am."

"I think we've underestimated you about a lot of things," Seth said quietly.

"Yeah, you have."

Seth decided to change the subject. "When did you first meet your other family?"

It was amazing to Marcus that Seth seemed so accepting. He'd thought for sure that Seth felt the same way as Dean, but he'd clearly misjudged his empathy.

"It was the year after Ma died. I was too curious not to find them. I kept searching through the forest and ranged farther and farther." Marcus smiled as he remembered the day he'd first met them. "I was headed down the trail to where their camp is now and I heard a bird call. I didn't think anything of it. The next thing I knew, I was surrounded by four Indians. I'd done some studying of the Lakota language and tried it out. I attempted to tell them that I was friendly. My accent was horrible, and they laughed at me, but they got the point."

"Seems like people laugh at you a lot," Seth said with a smile. "You bring it on yourself, though, you know."

"I know. I don't mind most of the time. I like making people laugh."

Claire remained silent as Marcus continued his story. She was as interested in all of it as Seth was.

"So they took me back to their camp. I thought they were going to kill me. They took me to the chief's tipi and asked him what they should do with me. He told them to make me sit down. They weren't gentle about doing it. His name was Brown Stag. For the longest time, he just sat looking at me. Then he spoke to me in English, which shocked the heck out of me.

"He asked me why I was looking for them. I told him about Ma being forced by one of their braves and that I was curious about my other family. I told him that I didn't know the brave's name, and I asked if he knew who it was. Brown Stag nodded and his eyes were so kind. There was no animosity in them as he told me that one of their braves who had been killed some years before had bragged about it. His name was Little Crow."

"Brown Stag said that Little Crow had other children by two different women. That's common in their culture, and not thought of as something bad. Little Rabbit was one of his wives and she's He Who Runs and Black Fox's mother. Owl and Squirrel, my sister, are Snow River's kids. Squirrel has two boys. They're very good people, Seth. You'd like them."

"So did they accept you right off?" Seth asked.

"Yes, because Brown Stag was my grandfather."

"You are the grandchild of the late chief of the tribe?" Claire said, amazed.

"Yes." Marcus looked beseechingly at Seth. "Can you see why I would be petrified to tell you guys? After a while, it just seemed easier not to tell you. I'm so sorry, Seth. I hope you'll be able to forgive me someday. I know Dean won't."

Seth absorbed everything Marcus had told him. "I can't speak for Dean, but I'm not going to turn my back on you. Pa didn't. He knew that you weren't his biological son, but he still accepted you and raised you as his own. You're still my little brother and you always will be. It's not your fault that Ma was attacked and got pregnant with you. I'm still annoyed that you didn't tell us, but I spent all night putting myself in your shoes. Now that I've heard your story, I *can* understand why you did it."

"Thank you," Marcus said with tears in his eyes. "You don't know what that means to me."

"So you think I would like these people, huh?"

Marcus grinned. "I know you would. Do you want to meet them?"

"Yeah. I do. Pa always said my curiosity would get me killed, but I gotta meet this other family of yours."

Marcus got all excited. "Okay. We'll go whenever you want to. Just say the word."

Seth laughed at his enthusiasm. "Okay, calm down. You love them, don't you?"

"Yeah, I do. You will, too."

"More than us?" Seth asked.

"I have enough love for all of you," Marcus said.

"I can believe that about you. I just have one more question for you," Seth said.

Marcus paused a little nervously. "What is it?"

"Are you cookin'?"

Marcus laughed and got up. "I can. We gotta teach that wife of yours how to cook. Speaking of that, come with me, Claire. You might as well start learning now." He grabbed her hand and started leading her inside.

Seth saw a flash of something shiny on Claire's ring finger and

gripped her wrist. "Hold up!" He recognized their mother's engagement ring and gazed at Marcus. "Does this mean what I think it
means?"

"What do you think?" Marcus responded.

"I think it means there's gonna be a wedding soon."

"You're smarter than you look," Marcus quipped and then
ducked into the house before Seth could react.

CHAPTER 14

*A*s Marcus cooked for Seth, Claire changed back into her regular dress but didn't put all of her petticoats on. She'd gotten used to the freedom of the Indian dress and didn't want to be quite so encumbered when they rode to the ranch.

For a moment, she ran her fingers over all the books that lined the shelves and looked at the titles of a few that sat in stacks on the floor. She wondered if Marcus had read all of them and wouldn't have been surprised if he had. She was amazed at how intelligent he was and how much he had retained. That he was self-taught and could hold his own with her impressed her. She thought it a shame that he hadn't had the opportunity to attend college. He would excel in his classes, she knew.

Seth had offered to come with them so he could help calm any flare-ups. Marcus was unsure about taking Aiyana with them, but Seth said that Maddie could watch her at their place in case things got heated with Dean. He also offered to carry Aiyana so Marcus and Claire could ride double.

"Why? I have another horse," Marcus pointed out.

Claire looked at him and said, "Marcus, I can't ride alone."

"You're gonna have to learn. You never know when it's going to be necessary for you to do so. What if I'm not around?" he said.

Seth nodded. "He's right, Claire. Maddie learned, and you will, too. It just takes some practice."

She rolled her eyes and said, "Very well."

Marcus brought Arrow out of the barn. The black horse tossed his head and pawed at the ground, a sign that he was anxious to be off.

"Where's your saddle?" Claire asked.

"I don't need one," Marcus answered.

"You don't?"

"Nope. Let's get you up on that horse," Marcus said.

Claire went over to Rosie and stroked her neck. "Please don't make me fall off," she said.

Marcus stood close by, ready to offer assistance. Claire's mount was a little shaky, but altogether not too bad. She settled into the saddle and took up the reins. Marcus smiled up at her. "Well done."

"Don't praise me just yet. As long as I don't fall off, I'll consider it a job well done."

"We'll call it an auspicious start then," Marcus said.

Claire nodded. "Agreed."

Marcus gave her thigh a little squeeze and turned to his own horse. He took a couple of quick steps, then grabbed Arrow's mane and pulled himself up onto the horse's back. Seth shook his head and said, "That's amazing. I didn't know you could do that. Of course, there's a lot I still don't know."

Marcus avoided his gaze and said, "In due time, Seth. In due time."

MADDIE WAS HANGING the washing on a long line. She would have never thought that she would enjoy chores like washing clothes or cleaning, but she did. Her experience with sewing and embroidery came in handy, and she had made beautiful curtains for their house.

Tessa and Lydia both envied her talent and had gotten her to make them curtains, too. Her only problem with running a house was cooking, and she didn't know what to do about that. Though she had taken a few lessons from her family's cook back home, the lessons didn't seem applicable to ranch-style food.

Tessa had tried to teach her, but though she'd listened and practiced and made notes, it hadn't seemed to make a difference. She felt bad about it, but Seth kept reassuring her that it wasn't a big deal. Maddie knew he sometimes ate at Dean's house, but she didn't mind. Seth was a big eater, and she cared that he got enough to eat. She also ate over there quite often.

As she put clothespins on a shirt, she smiled as she thought about the tiny life growing inside her. She knew Marcus was to thank for that. Her smile faded as her thoughts turned to the terrible events of the previous evening. All of them had been stunned over Marcus's incredible news, but Dean's reaction had been frightening. She hadn't witnessed it, but when Tessa had recounted it to her over breakfast that morning, her shock had been profound.

Dean was honest, reliable, and usually good-natured. He'd always been kind to Maddie, and she could see how much he loved his wife and children. The ranch wouldn't have kept going without all the hard work he put into it while Seth was away. He was a good provider and a good brother to his siblings. There had been times when he was annoyed with Marcus, but she didn't understand where the sudden rage at Marcus had come from.

She knew that Dean had been angry with Marcus even before he'd found Claire and him in the tack room. There was something that didn't add up about her little sister and brother-in-law's suddenly amorous relationship. She felt that Seth was right about that. Then her smile returned as she remembered how precious Marcus's baby was. His face had glowed with pride as he'd held and played with her. He was a natural father.

Maddie finished hanging the laundry and was on her way back inside when Seth, Marcus, and Claire came riding up the lane. She stopped and watched the procession. Seth was carrying something on his back. As they got closer, Maddie realized it was the cradleboard in which Marcus carried his baby.

She put a hand to her mouth to hide her laughter. Her husband looked funny with it on his back. They stopped in front of her, and Seth said, "Hey, good-lookin'. You wanna watch an Indian baby for a while?"

Maddie's face lit up. "I'd love to!"

Seth swung out of the saddle as Marcus helped Claire down. Claire put up a fuss over Marcus doing so, arguing that she had got up there so she guessed she could get down. Seth walked over to Maddie and planted a kiss on her full mouth, then he carefully took off the cradleboard and brought it around so that she could take Aiyana from it.

Maddie was able to get a good look at the baby in the light of day. "Oh my! She's beautiful! And she looks so much like her pa."

"Don't she?" Seth said. "I told Claire and Marcus about our good news. They were real excited about it."

"So am I," Maddie said, her eyes shining with happiness. Seth kissed her again.

Marcus approached them hesitantly. He knew Seth's position on the situation, but he didn't know what Maddie thought. He needn't have worried.

"Marcus, she is such a little angel! Look at the mischief in those eyes. You're going to have your hands full with her," Maddie said and kissed his cheek.

He looked a little bashful. "Thanks."

"Marcus, did you really think that I would think any less of you because you happen to be half Indian?" she asked.

Marcus shrugged. "There's a lot of bigotry about that, against them, and I didn't know how any of you would feel if you knew that I shared that heritage."

"You're still the Marcus I know and love. And, it's even better having you in my life now because you come with an adorable little girl!"

That made Marcus smile. "You say the nicest things, Maddie."

"It's true," Maddie said.

Seth took Claire's left hand and held it out for Maddie to see. "We're not the only ones with good news."

Maddie's eyes widened, and she handed Aiyana to Marcus in order to hug Claire. The two women rejoiced and Maddie kept looking at the engagement ring and hugging Claire. Then she turned to Marcus and embraced him.

"I won't say welcome to the family because you already are my family, but I'm so happy for you and Claire. I know you'll both be very happy," she said despite her niggling doubts.

No sooner had Marcus thanked her than she grabbed Claire's hand and started pulling her toward Dean's house. "We have to tell Tessa." Then she stopped and came back and took Aiyana from Marcus. "And we have to show Aiyana to her, too." With that, the two women were on their way to give Tessa all the good news, leaving Seth and Marcus to shrug and smile.

"I think it's a woman thing," Seth said.

"Must be. Well, I should get my stuff. At least some of it. Darn, I didn't think about not having a wagon," Marcus said.

"You have a wagon. It's in the barn," Seth said.

"No. That belongs to the ranch. I didn't buy it."

"You're right. We all bought it. You still own a third of this place, Marcus," Seth said. "C'mon."

He started toward the barn. Marcus was about to follow when he saw Dean come out of it. They stared at each other for a long moment, neither budging. Dean realized that Marcus wasn't afraid of him. That was fine with him.

"Dean, don't start anything," Seth said gently. "He doesn't have to, but he's come to get his stuff. There oughta be a way to work all this out. You're being an idiot, Dean."

"Do what you want, Seth. If you want to socialize with a liar, fine by me, but don't expect me to do it."

Marcus felt his heart crack a little more, but didn't give in to the pain. "Dean, won't you even try to understand? Pa didn't think any less of me, why do you?"

Dean walked right up to Marcus, and Seth got ready to intercede if necessary.

"Marcus, my problem has nothing to do with you being half Indian. It's the fact that you didn't tell us for so long. That's what hurts. After Ma died, I took care of you and Seth and I taught you everything we knew about ranching. We looked after you, cared about you." Dean's voice cracked. "We loved you. And you stabbed us in the back by keeping secrets and telling lies. That was something I thought we didn't do to each other. And if that's not bad enough, you tell us that you have this Indian family. Even that wouldn't be so bad, but *they* know about *us*. You didn't keep us a secret from them."

"Dean, it was different."

"Yeah, it sure was. As you would say, you didn't afford us the same courtesy as you did them. You thought more of them than you did us." Dean's nostrils flared. "I can't trust you, Marcus. I thought I knew you, but I don't. Not really. I'm sure that what you told us last night doesn't even begin to cover the number of things we don't know about you."

Marcus nodded. "You're right. There's a whole ocean of information I want to tell you because I want you to know all of me. I *want* you to know. Finding out that I have a daughter has freed me and given me the courage to do what I should have done long before now. Trust goes both ways, though. I trusted you with my secrets now because I thought that deep down you'd see my side and be willing to listen. I guess we were both wrong."

He stepped even closer to Dean. "And regarding my daughter? If you ever do anything that even remotely puts her in danger again, you'll regret it. She is completely innocent in all this and you throwing dishes and stuff around last night was reckless. She could have been seriously hurt. You've always accused me of being reckless and I am, but not when it involves someone else's life. You keep that in mind. I'm getting my stuff now and borrowing the wagon. I'll have it and the team back before sundown."

Marcus turned and walked into the barn. Dean looked at Seth. "So you're really on his side?"

Seth shook his head. "I'm not on his side, Dean. I'm on the side of what's right. It just so happens that you're not on that side right now. You're right. There's a lot more he has to tell. He told me some this morning, but I'm not going to tell you anything. When you're ready, you sit down with him and talk. That's what Pa and Ma would want us to do. Oh, and by the way? He and Claire are engaged now, so you act happy about it for Claire's sake because if you hurt her feelings, Marcus won't be the only one who's kicked your behind."

Dean was seething with anger as he watched Seth walk away. He stayed away from the barn, though. Instead, he walked through one of the pastures to a stand of trees. He sat down in their shade and began turning things over in his mind.

CHAPTER 15

Geoffrey O'Connor entered the family home in the Shady Side neighborhood of Pittsburgh. As he came into the foyer, he checked the mail. It was always put in a basket on a table near the door. There were several envelopes in the basket and he picked them all up. He was hoping for some news from his daughters, but there was no letter from any of his girls. There was, however, a letter from Marcus Samuels.

Geoffrey's eyebrows rose as he noted the formal way in which the letter was addressed. The letter had been sent to both him and Maureen, so he went in search of his wife. Mrs. Duncan, their head housekeeper, informed him that she was in their garden.

"There you are," Geoffrey said when he saw Maureen strolling along by her rose bushes.

Maureen turned and smiled, and Geoffrey was struck by her beauty, which hadn't diminished over the years. "Hello, Geoffrey. How was your day?"

Geoffrey kissed her. "Fine, and yours?"

Maureen's smile slipped a little. "I miss our girls, Geoffrey. I feel so alone here."

Geoffrey hugged her close. "I feel the same way. I was hoping for a letter from them, but there wasn't one." He released her and said, "However, Marcus has sent us a letter."

"Marcus? I wonder what that's about."

"Let's sit down on the bench and find out, shall we?"

"Yes."

They sat, and Geoffrey opened the letter. He read the letter aloud.

"Dear Mr. and Mrs. O'Connor,

"I hope this letter finds you both well. I send this letter because I have much to tell you and something to ask you. I hope that you will not think less of me when you read this. My identity is not quite what I have led everyone to believe. When I was sixteen, I discovered that Ralph Samuels was not my biological father. My biological father was an Indian brave from a local Lakota Indian tribe who raped my mother. I know this is shocking, but I beg you to please bear with me."

Maureen uttered a gasp of surprise. "How horrible for his mother," she said. She instantly thought of Maddie and was grateful that things hadn't gotten that far when Theo had attacked her.

Although he was as affected as Maureen by Marcus's revelation, Geoffrey continued reading.

"My mother kept journals and after she passed, I found them. While reading them, I found out the truth about my heritage. I have known for thirteen years, but I have been unable to tell my White family for fear that I would lose them. My family now knows, and while most have been accepting, it has caused a deep rift between Dean and me. I don't know that it will ever be repaired.

"I have other siblings from the Lakota tribe with whom I have good relationships. They know about my White family and do not hold any animosity toward me or them. I also recently found out that I have a daughter by an Indian woman named Redtail. We spent time together early last year, and she is the result of that liaison. You have to understand that in the Lakota culture, these kinds of relationships are not looked down upon. Redtail was killed in a Cheyenne raid almost two weeks before the time I'm writing this letter. My brothers, He Who Runs and Black Fox, brought Aiyana to

me. Aiyana means 'eternal blossom' in Lakota. She has my eyes, and she is beautiful.

"I hope now that you know the truth about me, you will not think any less of me and realize that I am still the same man you met and that my heritage is a positive part of me. There is much more to tell about all this, but I prefer to do that in person.

"Now, on to the main reason that I am writing this letter. As you know, Claire and I have been writing ever since Maddie and Seth's wedding. Our relationship began with much conflict. Over time, we grew to respect each other and appreciate each other's unique perspective on many subjects. We challenged each other and pushed each other to work and study harder. It made us better students, and I like to think that, in some small way, I helped Claire to achieve her degree. I am very proud of her for her accomplishments and do regret that I was unable to attend her graduation ceremony.

"Our letters became less contentious the longer we wrote, and we began exchanging personal information about our respective lives. Since Claire has been here, I've discovered what a charming and kind person she has become. Don't get me wrong, we still push each other, but there is no longer any real animosity between us.

"We have developed strong feelings for each other. I have asked her to marry me, and she has accepted my proposal. I know that it is traditional to ask the lady's father before proposing, but I'm an impetuous person and I could not wait to ask her. I am asking both of you for your blessing. It would mean so much to us if you were to give it."

Geoffrey and Maureen looked at each other in disbelief. "I certainly didn't see that coming," Geoffrey muttered. As a father, he was torn between disappointment at Marcus's lack of adherence to tradition and respect for his letter asking for their pardon and their blessing.

"Nor I. I always thought they only wrote to irritate each other," Maureen admitted honestly.

Something bothered her, but she couldn't quite put a finger on what it was. Tessa had run away to pursue her own dreams and to have an adventure. Her instinct to meet Dean with the possible intent of marrying had been a good one. Maureen and Geoffrey loved Dean and all of his children. That Dean loved Tessa and their family was evident whenever Geoffrey and Maureen were in Montana.

Maddie and Seth's circumstances were quite different. They had helped each other through some very difficult times. Geoffrey and Maureen had been witnesses to their deepening relationship. It had been a pleasure for Maureen and Geoffrey to watch their second daughter wed such a special man as Seth.

But this situation with Claire and Marcus was another matter. It confused her, and she could tell that Geoffrey was thinking along the same lines. His brow puckered, and he fiddled with his wedding ring, which was his habit when he was deep in thought. He raised the letter again and continued.

"I am not rich, but I make a decent living. My house is not large, but I keep it in good repair and together we would make it a home. I have quite a bit of land, so expanding wouldn't be a problem. On my honor, I will take good care of your daughter and make her happy in every way. Claire adores Aiyana and wants to help me raise her, and we plan on having more children.

"As I close this letter, I would respectfully ask that you consider your answer carefully and see that Claire and I make a good match and would have a happy life together.

"Respectfully, Marcus E. Samuels

"P.S. I look forward to dancing with you, Maureen, at the reception. Geoffrey, I know that you will be gracious and allow me this small pleasure."

Despite the serious nature of the letter, Geoffrey and Maureen smiled at Marcus's postscript. It was just like him to add some levity to break the tension a serious situation like this caused.

They looked at each other in silence for a few moments.

"What do you think, Maureen?" Geoffrey asked.

Maureen sighed. "I honestly don't know what to think. It's all rather sudden, but then again, neither of our other daughters' courtships was very long."

Geoffrey nodded. "You're right. Marcus is a good fellow. His moods can change on a dime, but Claire is much the same way. They're both highly intelligent and enjoy arguing about a variety of things. This whole new side to Marcus does give me pause. I've never had any dealings with Native Americans, so I'm not sure what to expect there. It would seem that Claire accepts his other family, however. Perhaps we should write a letter to Tessa and get her take on all of this?"

"I think that's a good idea," Maureen said.

IT DIDN'T TAKE LONG for Tessa to respond to their inquiries.

Dear Mama and Papa,

It was so good to hear from you! I miss you both so much and always enjoy hearing from you. Everyone here is well, but as Marcus stated in his letter to you, there has been much conflict over the revelations about his heredity.

I love my husband so much, but he is wrong about all of this. I can understand why he was so hurt about Marcus's deception, but he will not even attempt to take a look at the reasons that Marcus felt he could not come forward about it all. I cannot imagine what it must be like for Marcus to know that he is the product of such an awful event, and yet he is such a caring, amusing man.

When he first discovered this information, he feared being rejected by his brothers. At that time, he didn't know anything about his Lakota family, as he calls them, and would have had no one if Dean and Seth had disowned him. At the tender age of sixteen, this would have been an incredibly difficult burden to bear. I admire his fortitude in dealing with it all.

Although he won't admit it, Dean is also jealous of Marcus's other siblings and the close relationship that Marcus has with them. Seth says that he is going to take Marcus up on his offer to meet them. He is extremely curious about this other family and even though he is a little jealous, he has kept an open mind about it all.

Claire has already met several of Marcus's family and has developed an immediate rapport with them.

Marcus's daughter, Aiyana, is a joy. She has Marcus's beautiful gray eyes and his smile. I do not know much about her mother, but from what I can tell, Aiyana has Marcus's pleasant disposition. You will enjoy having her as a grandchild as much as you do Sadie and Jack. Marcus has always had an affinity for children and this is even more apparent when he is holding or playing with his daughter. He is extremely proud of her and is an excellent father.

It's amazing to see how nonchalant he is about changing diapers or cleaning up spit-up. He was the same with his niece and nephews, and I suspect that he has also done this a lot with his Lakota family. There are so many things about Marcus that make more sense now that we know his heritage. His appearance is only one of them.

Though he does not have a medical degree per se, he also has much medical training and has ministered not only to his tribe but to us as well. He has helped all of us with various ailments and injuries over the past few years and has most recently helped me through a very virulent period of morning sickness.

Regarding his and Claire's relationship, we were as confused as you about the sudden turnabout. While we still have questions, it's undeniable that they are close. It is not the closeness of friends, but rather a romantic intimacy. I do not think that Marcus, as impulsive as he can be, would have given his mother's engagement ring to Claire unless he was committed to her and had the utmost serious intentions toward her.

It is a beautiful emerald ring of excellent quality and Claire loves it so. This is mainly because of the significance of Marcus giving her something that obviously means a great deal to him. Personally, I think that they will make a good match. Frankly, I have always thought so. They already have our blessings, but I know that yours is the most important to them. I hope all this has helped you make up your minds.

All my love,
Tessa

P.S. One last bit of information about Marcus; he is a good cook, so they will not starve.

~

THE NEXT FEW days were busy ones for everyone. Claire made Marcus understand that his house needed a huge amount of work. Seth had laughed at Marcus's dismay as he and Maddie helped the younger couple clean out the place. Privately, he teased Marcus about learning to live with a woman.

"You're not gonna be able to leave your clothes all over the place like you're used to doing." Seth's brow furrowed. "Why *are* so many of your clothes on the floor?"

Marcus shrugged. "That's where I leave them when I go to bed."

"On the floor?"

"Yeah."

"Okay. Where are your underclothes?" Seth asked.

"On the floor."

"What do you wear to bed?"

"My skin," Marcus said with a smile.

"You sleep naked?"

"Now you're getting it," Marcus said with pride.

Seth's laugh rang through the small house. "You're gonna have to stop that, little brother."

"Why?"

"What if something unexpected happens?"

A cheeky smile spread across Marcus's face. "I'm counting on it."

Seth smacked his chest. "Knock that off. I meant outside. At least if you have pants on, you're prepared."

"If a bear comes around, do you really think pants are going to protect me? I have this thing they call a gun. That will protect me and mine much better than pants," Marcus said. "Besides, I don't think Claire is gonna mind."

Seth quit the conversation at that point, saying he didn't want to know any more than Marcus had imparted. Marcus laughed him out the door.

~

FOUR DAYS LATER, Seth was helping Marcus organize his barn. At one point, he turned around and was surprised to come face to face with an Indian brave. He hadn't heard the brave come up behind him. Seth eyed him for a moment, then smiled and said, "Which one are you? Black Fox, He Who Runs, or Owl?"

Surprise showed in the brave's dark eyes. "He Who Runs. Are you Dean?"

"Nope. Seth." Seth held out a hand.

He Who Runs looked at it a second and then shook hands with Seth.

"Nice to meet you," Seth said.

Marcus came into the barn and stopped when he saw the two of them. He said something in Lakota to He Who Runs, who smiled.

"What did you tell him?" Seth asked.

Marcus smiled. "I told him that you're very curious about them and that you're afraid to sleep naked."

Seth glowered at Marcus and stepped toward him. He Who Runs put a hand on Seth's chest and said, "That is not a good idea."

Marcus snapped something at him in Lakota and made a motion for He Who Runs to leave. The brave glowered at Seth.

"I'm not gonna hurt him," Seth said. He understood that He Who Runs was being protective. "We just clown around like that. Tell him, Marcus, I don't think he understands."

Marcus translated and He Who Runs smiled and dropped his hand. "So it is with you like it is us?"

Seth nodded. "Yep. Especially because he has such a smart mouth."

"I agree," He Who Runs said.

Marcus threw up his hands. "Great, now I'm going to have five brothers ganging up on me all at once."

"I think he is drunk," He Who Runs said. "There are only two of us here and yet he says five."

Seth laughed. "I think you're right."

Marcus left the barn, mumbling something about being the baby of both families. Seth and He Who Runs laughed harder over that.

After that, Marcus's other Lakota brothers bugged him so much about meeting Seth that he went to the ranch to get Seth. He rode up the lane, stopped Rosie outside Seth's house, and whistled for him.

Seth came from the direction of the barn. "Hey, Marcus, what brings you?"

"Your presence is requested at my house. Where's Claire? I came to get her, too. You know, I don't see what the big deal is about her staying at my place now instead of after the wedding."

Seth laughed. "Have you met Geoffrey O'Connor? He's the big deal and, trust me, you don't want to get on his bad side, especially if it involves his daughters. Now, who wants me at your house?"

"All of my Lakota brothers. They've been there the last couple of days, but you've been busy here. Can you come today? They're being real pains in my rear."

Just then, Claire came out onto Seth's porch. Marcus's face lit up at the sight of her, and she gave him a coy smile.

Seth watched the exchange as Marcus rode toward her. Under his breath, he muttered, "He ain't gonna make it until the wedding. Oh, boy."

WHEN SETH MET Marcus's other two brothers, he understood why it didn't bother Marcus to sleep naked. All three braves were dressed in only their loincloths and various pieces of jewelry. He Who Runs smiled at Seth and came forward. "Hello, brother."

Seth smiled as he dismounted and said, "Hello, brother." Marcus had told him that was the standard greeting among Lakota men, not necessarily blood brothers, but it still made him feel good that He Who Runs viewed him that way.

He was introduced to Black Fox and Owl. Seth had to look a second time at Owl. He looked a lot like Marcus. "Hello, brothers," Seth said.

Owl smiled, and he looked even more like Marcus. "Hello, brother. I am Owl."

Suddenly, He Who Runs tipped forward and almost went down. Marcus had come up behind him and tripped him. He laughed as He Who Runs turned to face him.

"Gotcha," Marcus said. "You gotta listen better than that, brother."

He Who Runs silently circled around Marcus, waiting for an opening. Black Fox and Owl backed off and left them to their wrestling. He Who Runs feinted, but Marcus was ready and countered the move with one of his own. Seth took comfort in the fact that Black Fox and Owl were smiling at the pair. After several minutes, Marcus raised his hands and said, "Okay. Enough, I gotta get to work here. You can avenge your honor later, He Who Runs."

Marcus's Indian brother smiled and then dropped and tried the same move Marcus had used on Dean. Marcus jumped at the last minute and avoided him. He Who Runs rolled over, caught Marcus's wrist, and brought Marcus down with him. There was a lot of grunting and laughing as they rolled around.

Seth couldn't tell who was winning, but it sure looked funny. Finally, the two men broke apart and stood up. Then they shook hands and patted each other's backs. Marcus came over to Seth. "So how did you like watching your first Lakota wrestling match?" His breathing was labored from the exertion.

"It was entertaining. I'd like to know how to do some of that," Seth said.

"Oh, hang around with us long enough and you will," Marcus said. "You'll get inducted into the club."

"Can't you just talk normal?" Seth said.

"I mean, you won't be able to help it. Once they know you well enough, you won't have a choice in the matter. You'll either learn or they'll wreak havoc on you."

"Really?" Seth said, eyeing them critically.

"Really," Marcus said. "Okay, I have to get to work here. My bride-to-be is already in the house and if I don't get to it, there'll be heck to pay."

"You better get used to it, little brother!" Seth said.

Marcus's Lakota brothers laughed because they knew it was the truth.

DEAN WAS FINDING out just how much work Marcus had done on the ranch. Not only had he repaired equipment and property but he'd also helped Maddie and Tessa with many things. He'd hauled water for washing clothes, chopped firewood for the stoves and fireplaces, and watched the kids when necessary.

Hard as Dean tried, and even with Ray and Marty's help, he was falling behind on the work. Seth had picked up some of the slack, but he was helping Marcus get his place sorted out so it was ready for after Claire and he were married. Jack wanted to help out more, but Dean didn't want to overwork the boy. However, he did insist that Sadie help Tessa more now that Tessa was getting further along in her pregnancy.

Marcus's absence was felt by everyone. Although part of it was because they needed his help, it was the loss of all the fun Marcus brought to the place that hurt the most. His whistling and laughter were missed. Dean kept trying to come to grips with it all, but his pride just wouldn't let him get over it.

Despite his jealousy, Dean was curious about Marcus's other family. He knew through Tessa and Jack that Seth had met a few of them and liked them. This further outraged him because he felt like Seth was choosing sides. He was thinking about all of this as he sat at the kitchen table going over some paperwork late one night.

Dean heard hoofbeats and then a whistle that was reserved only for him. Marcus had come up with a different whistle for each family member. Out of habit, he smiled and then remembered that he was angry and hurt. His smile disappeared when the whistle was repeated. Dean tried to ignore it, but it came again, even louder. He let out an exasperated sigh and headed outside.

"What is it, Marcus? I'm busy."

"I'm sure you are, but I have something important to discuss with you. Can you come over here?" Marcus asked.

"Why can't I stay right here?" Dean said.

"Well, you told me not to darken your doorstep again, and I want to make sure my shadow doesn't fall on it," Marcus explained.

Dean almost smiled at Marcus's sarcastic remark, but he was able to hold it back at the last second.

"C'mon, Dean. That was funny. Okay, I'll come to you so I don't have to shout," Marcus said, moving closer.

As he looked into Marcus's eyes, Dean realized how much he'd missed Marcus and he had trouble keeping tears out of his eyes. "What is it?"

"You know I'm getting married soon, right?"

"Yes, I know."

Marcus shuffled his feet a little. "I know how you feel about me right now, but I still want you to stand up with me. I know you won't be my best man even though you were my first choice. Seth understands why that is, and he has graciously agreed to step up if you won't do it. I'm not asking for your answer right this moment, but I'd like you to at least think about it. Will you do that much?"

Dean swallowed his immediate reply and instead asked, "What about your other brothers? Why don't you ask one of them?"

Marcus smiled. "Oh, they'll be there, but they don't want to stand up in front of everyone in a suit. They don't look any better in a suit than you and Seth would in loincloths. Can you imagine Seth in a loincloth? Maddie might like it, though."

Dean couldn't resist smiling at that image. "Yeah, that would be something to see."

"There's that smile I miss so much! So, you'll think about it?" Marcus asked. "Just think about it? The fact is, Dean, I've always looked up to you. I harass you all the time about being so serious and working too hard, but I've learned how to be a good husband from you. I remember some stuff about Pa, but I was only fourteen when he died. You're the one I've watched all these years, Dean. First, it was with Sarah and now it's with Tessa. I've also learned what it means to be a good father and not just the fun uncle, and that sometimes you have to be a father and not a friend. Okay, well that's all I wanted to say. Just think about it."

Marcus went back to Arrow and mounted him. "Oh, and Dean?"

"Yeah?"

"You don't have to talk to Jack about that subject that's so embarrassing for you. I already did it for you." With that, he turned and rode away.

Dean was so astonished at that last bit of information that he just stood gaping after him for several minutes.

CHAPTER 16

*M*addie heard yelling from the drive by the barn and hurried out of the kitchen only to run smack into Seth. He steadied her and said, "Sorry, honey. You gotta come see this."

Maddie followed her husband onto the porch and saw Marcus and Claire arguing. It was something about plants and hybrids, but it was past her comprehension.

"All right. They're arguing. What's so exciting about that, Seth? They do it all the time." She was slightly annoyed because she wanted to get the dishes done.

"Shh!" Seth said as Marcus turned to walk away from Claire. "Watch this."

Maddie's brow knitted in response to Seth shushing her, but she did what he asked.

Even as Marcus walked away from Claire, he kept up the disagreement. Claire's mouth never shut either as she followed him. The next thing they knew, Claire caught up to Marcus and grabbed a fistful of his hair. Marcus groaned and turned around. Maddie would have interceded, but Seth stopped her.

"Just watch."

Marcus grabbed Claire's waist and hauled her to him and planted a hard kiss on her mouth. When he released her, they were both smiling. Then they resumed the arguing, but Marcus made sure to keep out of Claire's reach.

"It's the oddest thing, Maddie. It happens every time she pulls his hair, and she does it a lot," Seth said. "The first time I saw it happen, I thought for sure that he was gonna do something to her, but he just kissed her and then they got all mushy like that."

Maddie reached up and yanked on Seth's hair.

"Ow! What did you do that for?"

"Just experimenting," Maddie said with a laugh.

CLAIRE STOOD BACK from the window and looked at it with a critical eye. Marcus stepped down from a stool he was standing on so he could hang them and said, "They look great, Maddie."

"Thank you," Maddie said. She had made curtains and was nervous about what Claire thought about them.

"My fiancé is right," Claire said with a huge smile at Maddie. She hugged and kissed Maddie. "Thank you so much for all of your help."

"You're welcome. Curtains add the finish to any room," Maddie said.

Claire gave Marcus a wry look. "Tell him that."

Marcus shrugged. "I've never decorated, so I don't know anything about it."

"That's obvious," Claire said.

"Hey, I warned you that I wasn't good at everything. This is one of those things," Marcus said. "So when I tell you to do whatever you want with the place, I'm not being blasé, I'm admitting that you're best equipped to do the job. I'll help with whatever you want, but you're gonna have to guide me."

Claire smiled. "So, you're admitting that I'm smarter than you?"

"I'm admitting no such thing. I'm simply saying that in this particular area, I'm not experienced and it's better left to you," Marcus said.

"Well, at least you're honest," Maddie said.

"I try. The only request I have is that you don't reorganize my medicine and spices in the kitchen," he said to Claire.

"Why?"

"Because if you were to accidentally use the wrong thing when you're cooking, it could kill you," Marcus said matter-of-factly.

Maddie and Claire looked at each other and smiled.

"Ladies, I'm being completely serious. Certain plants are poisonous if they're not used correctly, so please don't rearrange it, Claire," Marcus explained. His voice and face were devoid of all humor.

"Very well," Claire said. "I won't."

"Thanks." Then Marcus was all smiles again as he said, "So what's next on the list?"

"Well, I think we do need to reorganize the cupboards so there's room for actual dishes," Maddie said. As she turned toward the kitchen, she uttered a short cry of fear.

Black Fox was standing in the doorway between the parlor and kitchen. Maddie was rooted to the spot. She'd never seen anyone like him before and was scared speechless. Claire, however, went right over to Black Fox and hugged him.

"Hello, brother," she said.

Black Fox wasn't a big hugger, but he returned Claire's embrace. "Hello, sister."

"Black Fox, this is my sister, Maddie."

"Hello, Maddie," he said.

Maddie finally found her voice. "Hello, Black Fox."

Marcus watched them with amusement. Black Fox said something to him in Lakota that made him smile even more broadly.

"What did he say?" Maddie asked.

"He said that he sees why Seth loves you so much. You're a beautiful woman," Marcus answered.

Maddie blushed. "Thank you."

Black Fox started looking around the house and laughed. "Silver Ghost is becoming tamed, I think," he remarked wryly.

Marcus smirked at his brother and said, "You're just jealous because I can keep warmer in the winter than you and I have more room."

"I keep warm just fine," Black Fox with a wink at Maddie. "I hear you do, too." Then he left.

Marcus looked at where Black Fox had just been and then back at Maddie.

"Just what is my husband telling him?" she asked.

Marcus shrugged. "I have no idea."

"I'm going to go find out," she said. She turned and stomped out of the house.

"What about the cupboards?" Claire called after her.

THE NIGHT BEFORE THE WEDDING, Claire lay wide awake in her bed in Seth and Maddie's house. She was nervous and happy. Soon, she would be marrying the man of her dreams, the man she'd loved for three years. She couldn't believe it sometimes. There were nights when she had nightmares that he was gone and she was left alone.

Then she'd see him the next day and all of her fears would abate. He'd assigned a whistle to her just as he had the rest of the family members. She would hear it and rush outside to find him waiting with a smile on his face. Her heartbeat would skitter in her chest and she'd feel warm all over.

Then he would say something smart and irritate her. Just when she was getting angry, he'd compliment her on something. She had found out what Seth had meant when he'd told her that she would have her hands full with Marcus. He could be charming, annoying, and kind all in a matter of minutes, and sometimes she didn't know if she was coming or going.

He knew it, too. There were times when she thought it was no wonder that people got annoyed with him. There were also times

when she understood why they all loved him. She saw that he sometimes purposely made himself the butt of a joke and acted offended
to make other people laugh.

Claire had also come to know what passion felt like. She couldn't
seem to help herself around him. For all of his good humor, there
was something virile and intoxicating about him that made her crave
his touch.

Regarding the redecorating of his house, he'd been true to his
word and left her to do almost anything she wanted except for
anything with his medicine and spice rack. He was also very protective of her and had shown that on a couple of occasions when they
were in his family's camp.

Claire had been gathering some kindling for a fire one morning
when a young brave had surprised her. He had made inappropriate
advances toward her. She'd rebuffed him, but he wasn't getting the
hint. Marcus had snuck up behind him and grabbed him from behind.
He'd held a knife to the brave's throat and warned him that if he ever
came near Claire again, he'd slit his throat from ear to ear.

Then he'd pushed the brave away and kicked him in the backside
so hard he'd hit his head on a tree and fallen to the ground in a daze.
Marcus had rolled his shoulders and turned to Claire. She'd seen the
fierce light of battle in his eyes and had been a trifle scared. Then he
had blinked and smiled and he was her sweet, funny man again.

Claire looked at her engagement ring as the moonlight caught it
and was reminded of the night Marcus had proposed to her. He
hadn't said that he loved her, but that hadn't mattered to her at the
time. She'd told Tessa about being disappointed that Marcus hadn't
said the words to her yet, but Tessa had just chuckled and told her
not to worry.

It had been the same way with her when Dean had proposed. It
wasn't until later that Dean had declared his love for her, but it had
been worth waiting for. Tessa said to pay attention to the way Marcus
looked at her and the tone of his voice and she'd see his love. Still,
Claire hoped and prayed that she would actually hear the words
someday.

For now, though, she'd settle for becoming his wife and making a home with him and their daughter. She smiled as she thought about the little baby who she'd come to love so much. Marcus was very generous with his daughter and left some of her care to Claire when she was with them because he said it was a good experience for when they were married. He'd taught her so much about childcare and she knew that he had much more to teach her about a lot of things.

THAT SAME NIGHT, Marcus was sitting on his porch, whittling again. Aiyana was sleeping peacefully in the new cradle that Seth had made for her. Marcus whistled as he worked. His keen ears picked up the sound of a horse coming down the lane to his house. The horse snorted, and he recognized Twister's whicker.

Dean dismounted and dropped Twister's reins to the ground. The horse stayed in place as he was trained to do. When Dean stepped into the lantern light, Marcus smiled at him. "Hey, Dean. Have a seat. Want a drink?"

"Okay," Dean said. He took a seat next to Marcus.

"Be right back. Mind your niece for me, okay?" Marcus said, pointing to the cradle on the porch, before disappearing into his house.

Dean looked down at the baby and smiled. Everyone was right, she was adorable. As if sensing Dean was there, Aiyana woke up and looked at him. She gurgled happily and reached her arms out to him. Unable to resist her, Dean picked her up and put her on his lap. Her gray eyes watched him closely, and Dean saw Marcus's smile when her lips curved upwards. He laughed at the sight.

Marcus watched them from the doorway and felt his heart swell as Dean talked to the baby and told her how pretty she was. He went out onto the porch and placed Dean's drink on the porch floor next to his chair. Settling back into his own chair, he took a drink of the whiskey he'd poured and said, "So what do you think?"

"I'd say that you have one beautiful daughter, Marcus."

"Thank you," Marcus said.

Dean laid Aiyana back in her cradle, and Marcus gave her a rattle that Owl had made for her to play with. Instead of rattling it, Aiyana decided to chew on it.

Dean laughed, and Marcus was reminded of how much he missed his big brother. Dean relaxed in the chair and took a swig of his drink. He was silent for a little while. Marcus waited patiently; he knew that Dean sometimes had to work himself up to saying something and when he was quiet like that, it was usually something important.

Marcus had just put his drink down and picked up the piece of wood he was working on when Dean cleared his throat and said, "I wanted to thank you for talking to Jack for me. It's much appreciated. I'm trying to come to grips with all of this other stuff, Marcus, Lord knows I am, but I'm just not there yet."

He looked intently at Marcus, and Marcus knew what was coming next. "I just can't stand up with you tomorrow. I'm sorry." With that, he got up and left.

As Twister's hoofbeats faded away, Marcus leaned back in his chair. Tears trickled from the corners of his eyes.

CHAPTER 17

$\mathcal{U}$nlike his brothers, Marcus had no anxiety about the wedding that was going to begin momentarily. Instead of sweating with trepidation or playing with his suit, he kept winking at Maureen and entertaining everyone. Geoffrey and Maureen had given their blessing, which had overjoyed Claire and Marcus. When they'd arrived in Dawson and seen Claire and Marcus together, they'd known they'd made the right decision.

They'd also seen that Marcus and Claire's relationship was not dignified. They argued and played more than anyone they'd ever seen. The first time they'd been witness to the "hair-pulling thing" as Seth called it, Geoffrey's eyebrows had almost touched his hairline. Seth had laughed and told him, "It happens all the time. I don't know what it is. Maddie's pulled my hair a couple of times like that and it just hurts. It's weird."

They'd known that Marcus could be a clown, but they didn't realize just how much of one until they watched him with the kids. They liked to play tag and Marcus was rarely "it" because they couldn't catch him. He ran, rolled, or jumped to avoid their touch. They had never heard Claire laugh so much. Claire had forbidden anyone from telling Marcus her middle name and no matter how much he bugged her about it, she wouldn't tell him. It was just another one of the strange things about their relationship that only they understood.

One morning, Marcus surprised his future parents-in-law by showing up to cook breakfast at Seth and Maddie's home, where they were staying since tension still existed between Dean and Marcus. Geoffrey was impressed with his whistling and complimented him on it.

Marcus told him that he was whistling because he was wooing Maureen, and Geoffrey had just laughed. Then, when he knew the women were occupied making wedding plans, Geoffrey had whispered in Marcus's ear, "If you hurt my daughter in any way, shape, or form, I'll kill you. Understand, laddie?"

As a man who now had a daughter of his own, Marcus did understand and assured Geoffrey that he would take good care of Claire. Mollified, Geoffrey had gone back to being good-natured and Marcus had breathed a sigh of relief.

Marcus's Indian brothers were also attending the wedding. They sat in the back of the church and watched the people around them. They realized that Marcus had a lot of family on both sides. Dean was also sitting in the back. He wouldn't stand up with Marcus, but at least he'd shown up.

Black Fox and He Who Runs kept throwing him dark glances, which Dean returned. Marcus wasn't oblivious to the animosity and sent his Lakota brothers some sign language that told them he didn't want any trouble on his special day. After that, they ignored Dean.

Marcus's suit was not quite traditional. Instead of a tie, he was wearing an elaborate necklace of turquoise beads and gold. It was very ceremonial in appearance and perfectly suited him. Claire had insisted he blend his two cultures, and he had appreciated her thoughtfulness. At one point while he waited for Claire to appear,

Marcus almost started whistling, but Seth stepped lightly on his foot and said, "Not now, little brother."

They didn't have a flower girl, but Mikey served as their ring bearer and he did a splendid job of it. He gave Seth the rings with seriousness. Seth smiled, remembering how Mikey used to call him "Uncle Shush," and ruffled the little boy's dark hair as he left to go sit with his father.

∾

WHILE MARCUS WAS HAVING a good time, Claire was on the verge of panic. She was having doubts, not about her feelings for Marcus, but about her ability to make him happy, and her sisters had their hands full trying to calm her down. They were shocked at the way their normally intelligent sister was falling apart.

"What if I'm not a good wife? What if I don't please him? What if he hates my cooking or I don't wear something he likes? I don't know if I'm going to be good at gardening or sewing or anything!" she exclaimed with fear.

Maddie giggled at her and said, "Claire, we see the way he looks at you. I think he'll be happy with anything you do. He might argue with you, but the two of you like to argue, so it'll be fine."

"Listen to Maddie. Every bride feels like this, but as soon as you see him at that altar all of your fear will fade away. I promise," Tessa said.

Claire said, "Are you sure?"

Tessa hugged her and said, "Positive."

Then Geoffrey was there, and it was time to go.

∾

MARCUS WAS WATCHING Maureen play with Aiyana when Seth nudged him. He looked down the aisle and saw Claire. She was resplendent in her white dress. Marcus's gaze trailed over the way it fit her to perfection. Then he looked up and caught her eye. He saw the fear there and sought to assuage it. Claire saw that big smile of his and felt her anxiety begin to fade. When he arched an eyebrow at her and softly whistled her special whistle, she began to laugh a little and she was no longer afraid. Geoffrey sent Marcus an admonishing look, but Marcus's gaze was fixed on Claire's. Geoffrey looked at Seth, who just shrugged and rolled his eyes.

Maddie and Tessa, who were already at the altar, couldn't hide their smiles. Tessa was unsurprised that Marcus would act up even at his own wedding. Claire didn't mind and was grateful to him for helping relieve her nerves.

Geoffrey placed Claire's hand in Marcus's and gave him the same look he'd given Seth on his wedding day. Marcus's smile faded, and he became completely serious as he silently assured Geoffrey that he got the message.

Satisfied, Geoffrey kissed Claire and went to sit with Maureen and their newest granddaughter. Claire felt like she was dreaming as they recited their vows. The congregation was surprised when Marcus said, "I take you, Claire I-still-don't-know-your-middle-name Fawn O'Connor, to be my lawfully wedded wife."

Claire had wanted him to say it like that and Marcus happily obliged. As he said it, her shoulders shook with laughter. They both had trouble getting through the rest of the vows. By the time it was over, the congregation was laughing with them. Marcus had begged Claire to not pull his hair when they kissed, but she couldn't resist tugging a little. They kissed until Seth broke them up.

The reception was a hilarious affair. Marcus and Claire danced the first dance. Seth had given Marcus a few dancing lessons and his little brother had caught on fairly quickly. Claire wasn't the best dancer, but she and Marcus made it through the dance with little trouble. Then Seth went over and asked Geoffrey to dance.

Geoffrey and Seth had planned the prank as soon as Geoffrey had arrived in Dawson. Geoffrey took Seth's hand, and they began to whirl around the floor together, much to the delight of their audience. Marcus laughed so hard he almost fell over. When they were done, Seth and Geoffrey took turns bowing and curtsying to each other.

Seth gave a very ineloquent speech. Every time he mentioned one of Claire's good qualities, he contrasted it by saying something negative about Marcus. This went on until Marcus put a stop to it. When the dinner was served, Claire cut up Marcus's food, much to his chagrin and everyone else's amusement. They had several little arguments about things, but when Marcus had enough, he kissed her instead of walking away.

As Dean and Tessa ate and danced, they remembered how they had decided to work on getting Marcus and Claire together. That plan had taken three years to come to fruition. It was a bittersweet feeling for Dean because of everything that had transpired over the past weeks. He was happy for Marcus and Claire, but he was still so angry and didn't even really know why.

Marcus was feeling the effects of the moonshine Black Fox had given him, so he went outside to get some fresh air. He didn't want to be drunk on his wedding night. He Who Runs followed him. "You are a lucky man, Silver Ghost."

"Don't I know it," Marcus said. "Thanks for coming today and staying for the reception. It means a lot to me."

He Who Runs put a hand on his shoulder and said, "It is an honor to attend your wedding to Fawn and I wish you many years of happiness."

"Thanks," Marcus said. "Are you leaving?"

"Yes. It is time. We will see you soon?" He Who Runs asked.

"You bet," Marcus replied. As he watched as his brother walked away, he sensed another presence beside him and said, "Hi, Dean."

"How'd you know it was me?" Dean asked.

"Your cologne. You're the only one who wears it," Marcus explained.

"Oh. Congratulations, Marcus. I'm very happy for you."

"That's nice of you to say," Marcus said. There was an edge to his words.

Dean looked at him. "I mean it."

Marcus nodded. "I know." He turned to face Dean. "I appreciate it, but I'm going to tell you something. If the situation had been in reverse, I would have still stood with you. I put my heart on the line when I asked you to just stand with me and you stomped on it. I won't be making that mistake again. Have a good night, Dean."

Dean blew out a breath as Marcus left. An Indian came to stand by him. "You are lucky to have a brother like Silver Ghost, Dean. Why not cherish him instead of hurting him?"

"Which one are you?" Dean asked.

"Black Fox. You have known him longer than we have and yet we do not hold it against you. We are not your enemy and neither is he. There is no reason for jealousy or anger. Do not waste time with such feelings."

Then Dean was left alone with his thoughts.

CLAIRE WAS LOOKING for her new husband when she saw him come in from outside. She could tell that he was agitated about something. His gray eyes were troubled and his shoulders were tense. She excused herself from Lydia and Charlie and went to him.

"Hello, dummy," she said. "Are you all right?"

"Yeah, I'm okay," he said with a smile. "Have I told you how beautiful you are?"

"Only about a hundred times, but I'm not complaining," Claire said. She wanted to help him with whatever was bothering him. "What's wrong?"

Marcus shrugged. "Dean. What else?"

Claire's heart went out to him and she silently cursed Dean. She crooked a finger at him and he bent down so she could whisper in his ear. "When we get out of here, I'll make you forget all about Dean."

He straightened and grinned at her, and she arched a brow at him. He took her hand, and they began saying their goodbyes. Marcus had asked her if she wanted to stay at the hotel in town, but she'd said she wanted to go to their house. Aiyana was being watched by Seth and Maddie. They kissed their daughter goodbye and then Marcus helped her into the two-wheeled buggy that they'd bought.

As they drove home, Marcus said, "Today was incredible."

Claire smiled at him. "Yes, it was. Can you believe Papa and Seth?"

Marcus laughed. "That was hysterical. I never expected that out of either of them. I wonder whose idea it was."

"We'll have to see if we can get them to tell us."

They spent the remainder of the ride reminiscing about the wedding and reception. When they pulled into the lane to their home, Marcus saw that Owl had carried out his request to follow them home and then cut through the woods to reach their house first and light the candles that Marcus had set around.

Warm light shone out of the windows. Marcus smiled when he heard Owl's familiar call and returned it with his own, saying good-night and thanks to his brother.

Claire recognized the call and shot Marcus a glance. "What was that about?"

"Just a little last well-wishing," he told her as they stopped in front of the house.

Marcus got out of the buggy and helped Claire down. He watched her go into the house, thinking how beautiful she was and that he was a lucky man. After putting Arrow away, he stepped into the parlor to be greeted by the most beautiful sight he'd ever seen. The candlelight somehow made it look like Claire had a halo, and he acknowledged that she really was his angel.

He smiled down into her eyes as the candlelight flickered in them. "Claire, tonight you can pull my hair as much as you want."

So she did.

CHAPTER 18

$\mathcal{C}$laire had thought being engaged to Marcus was fun, but being married to him was a hundred times more so. He made her breakfast almost every day and whistled the whole time he cooked. He talked a blue streak to Aiyana in both English and Lakota. She got to see him bathe in the stream that ran behind the house. He kept trying to get her to join him, but she was too bashful. She couldn't help peeking out the window at him, though.

She fell deeper in love with him every day. When they argued, Aiyana just laughed at them. More times than not, their arguing ended with them going to bed. Claire discovered that Marcus didn't require much sleep, but that when he did sleep, nothing could wake him. He regularly brought her flowers of all different varieties. There were times when he was bossy and declared that it was speaking-Lakota-only day.

Claire was caught up in a delicious whirlwind of love, romance, and passion. Aiyana grew more every day, and Claire loved the little girl deeply. Some nights when she woke up and their bed was empty, she found Marcus asleep on the sofa with Aiyana on his chest. The sight warmed her heart.

Marcus had found the perfect wife in Claire. She was sweet,

exciting and a great debater. He was impressed with her business knowledge. She had taken a look at their finances and figured out some ways to improve them that he hadn't thought of before. Claire was a fantastic mother to Aiyana, and their bond deepened every day. Marcus loved watching Claire play with the baby.

One day in early August, Seth came to their house and pounded on the door. When Claire opened it he said, "I need your husband. Now. Tessa's in labor and it's not going so well."

Claire instantly became alarmed. "What about Dr. Turner?"

"Too far away," Seth explained.

Marcus came out of their bedroom and said, "Hey, Seth. Did you come for supper?"

"No. We need you. Tessa needs you. She started labor a few hours ago and there's some kind of problem. Doc is too far away. Lydia's doing all she can, but something's not right."

Marcus turned to Claire. "Please put Aiyana in her cradleboard. I'll get a few things that should help."

Seth watched him begin putting jars from his medicine rack in a sack and wondered what they were for. When Claire had the baby ready and the cradleboard on her back, they went outside. Marcus whistled loudly, and Arrow circled around the pasture and jumped the fence. Marcus mounted the horse, and Seth helped Claire up.

"How are you gonna steer him?" Seth said.

"Knee and hand pressure. All Indian horses are taught that. Let's go."

~

EVEN BEFORE THEY ARRIVED, they could hear Tessa's cries of agony. Marcus laid his sack on the table and warned everyone not to touch it, then went into Dean and Tessa's bedroom. Tessa's hair was wet with sweat and she was crying with fear and pain. Dean was sitting beside her, holding her hand. He scowled at Marcus.

"What are you doing here?"

"I'm here to help Tessa and my niece. If you stay in this room, you better keep your mouth shut. I need to concentrate. You start on me and I'll have Seth throw you out." Then he turned and smiled at Tessa. "You just gotta be the center of attention, huh?"

Tessa laughed through her tears and she grabbed Marcus's hand. "Can you help?"

"Of course I can. I need to see what's going on here, okay?" Marcus said.

"Do whatever you need to do," Tessa said.

"I think the baby might be breech, but I can't seem to get it turned. It's stuck," Lydia said.

Marcus made a careful assessment of Tessa and the baby. "You're right. Tessa, don't push. No matter how much you want to, don't push." He ran out to the kitchen and quickly brewed three separate potions. He cooled them as quickly as he could and had Claire help him bring them back into the bedroom.

He sat down by Tessa and said, "Dean, help her sit up a little more. Tessa, you have to drink this. It'll help with the pain."

Dean supported Tessa as she drank. When she had finished, she sank back against the headboard and rested a little. Marcus waited a few minutes before giving her the next potion. "Next one. This is going to make you feel loopy. You may even sleep for a little, and that's a good thing."

Tessa drank again. It wasn't long before she became very relaxed and seemed to go to sleep.

Marcus jumped into action at that point. "If anyone's squeamish, look away now," he said. He'd wanted Tessa out of it somewhat so he could manually reach in and turn the baby. It was going to be very painful, and it was better that Tessa was semi-conscious so she didn't feel any more pain than necessary. Marcus manipulated the baby and got it into position. He was sweating and breathing heavily by the time he'd finished.

"Claire, bring that last potion here, please," he said.

Claire gave it to him, and Marcus had Dean help Tessa drink it. "That's going to help wake her up and bring on the contractions again."

Marcus patted Tessa's hand and kept talking to her about anything and everything just to get her more awake. When her eyes were a little clearer, he smiled at her and said, "Are you ready to get this little girl born?"

She nodded and gave him a weak smile.

"Dean, I want you to move into the bed with Tessa and get behind her. Let her push off you when the contractions come. When they do, you're also going to push down on her stomach. Get into position."

Dean hesitated for a moment before doing as directed. Marcus grabbed his hands and showed him exactly where to place them on Tessa's stomach. "Get ready, folks. It won't be long now."

Before long, Tessa's contractions started up again. Dean pushed when Marcus told him to, and Tessa's cries filled the room. Maddie, Seth, Jack, and Sadie paced nervously in the parlor. Lydia stayed close in case they needed something else. At last, the baby came sliding out and Marcus caught it.

He shouted with laughter. "Folks, you've got a beautiful little girl, just like I said." He snipped the umbilical cord and gave the baby to Lydia to be cleaned up. "Tessa, I know you're tired, but we have to do this one more time."

Dean gave Marcus a startled look. "What are you talking about?"

"Twins, Dean. There's another baby in there. That was part of the problem. I could tell when I turned the baby. That's why it took so long to get it turned. The second one should be in position, so it'll be easier." He kissed Tessa's cheek and said, "You can do it. You're a strong woman and you can do this."

Dean gathered Tessa back against him and kissed her hair. "Darlin', we gotta get this other baby born. It sure is a surprise, but a wonderful one. I love you so much. I'm right here. I'm gonna help you, okay?"

Tessa nodded, but then more contractions started and she grabbed Dean's arm as he bore gently down on her stomach as Marcus had shown him to do. Before much longer, Marcus held a baby boy in his arms. He handed him to Lydia and sat down heavily on the bed.

Exhaustion showed in his face. Lydia handed the little girl to Dean and the boy to Tessa, and sheer joy lit their faces.

"Congratulations," Marcus said.

Tessa reached out a hand to him. "Thank you, Marcus. We'll never be able to repay you."

Marcus smiled. "Just keep making those peach cobblers and we'll be even."

Tessa laughed and then turned her attention back to her new son. "Dean, why don't you take the babies out into the parlor while I get Tessa more presentable?" Lydia suggested.

Dean nodded, and Claire came forward to take the little boy from Tessa while Dean carried their little girl. As soon as they stepped into the parlor, everyone gathered around and congratulated Dean. Sadie took her new little sister from Dean and held her close for a little while. Then she handed her to Seth and left the house quickly.

Noticing her sudden exit, Dean gave his new son to Maddie and went after her. He found her in the barn. She was sitting on a hay bale, crying. Dean knelt before her and gathered her to him. "Sadie, honey, what's wrong? Mama's okay and so are the babies. Everything is all right."

"That's not it. I know they're all fine and I'm so happy about it." She raised her eyes to meet Dean's, and he saw that they were filled with misery. "Pa, I have to tell you something, but please don't throw me out."

Dean's face showed his alarm. "Sadie, I would never do that. What's all this about?"

"I'm pregnant, Pa," she whispered. "I'm going to have a baby."

Dean couldn't grasp what she was telling him. He held Sadie as she cried, struggling to comprehend what she'd said. "You're pregnant?" Anger started building in his chest, but he held it back. "Is it Tucker's?"

Sadie nodded and looked at him again. "Please don't kick me out like you did Uncle Marcus. I know we're young, but we love each other and he's got a good job at the feed mill in town. I'm good at sewing and can make money doing that for people." She took a ring from a dress pocket and showed it to Dean. "He asked me to marry him and I said yes. He's really happy about the baby. We both are. Please don't be angry, Pa. Please? I need you. *We* need you."

Dean thought back to when he'd married Sarah. They hadn't been much older than Tucker and Sadie. Sadie was seventeen now and Tucker was a year older. Dean knew the Fosters well, and they were a good family. Tucker was a good boy, and a responsible one at that. Sadie's remark about Marcus stung, and after what Marcus had just done for them, Dean felt a chink in the armor he'd put around his heart regarding his brother.

"Shh. It's okay, honey. I'm not mad. It'll be okay." He held his daughter and couldn't believe that she was all grown up and going to make Tessa and him grandparents when they'd just had twins. The irony of it struck Dean, and he started to laugh.

Sadie raised her head and looked at him with a confused smile. "Why are you laughing?"

Dean composed himself. "Well, I guess our kids will grow up together."

They laughed together for a while and then Dean said, "You tell that fiancé that he did things kinda backward and send him to see me for a talk, all right?"

Sadie smiled. "Okay. Please don't scare him too much, Pa."

"I'll be as nice as I can, but you're always gonna be my little girl and I want to protect you. That's all I've ever wanted to do, honey. I'm sorry we were fighting so much the past few months," Dean said.

"Me, too, Pa," Sadie said. "I love you."

Dean squeezed her and said, "I love you, too. Come on back in the house."

"I'd like to just sit here a little, Pa," Sadie said.

Dean looked into her eyes and said, "You sure?"

Sadie nodded, so Dean kissed her forehead and left her. As he walked back to the house, Dean felt like he'd aged a hundred years. So much had changed in such a short time. He'd just become the father of twins and now found out that he was going to be a grandfather. When he entered the kitchen, Seth was sitting in one of the chairs holding his newest niece.

Dean sat down by him and put his head in his hands.

Seth eyed his brother and asked, "What's wrong?"

"Tonight's been one heck of a night."

"Yep," Seth said with a smile at the baby. "It sure has."

"Sadie's pregnant," Dean blurted out.

That knocked Seth for a loop and he couldn't speak for a moment. "Oh, boy," he finally said. "Tucker's?"

"Yep."

"Well, Dean, I can't say that I didn't see it comin'," Seth said. "So what did you say?"

Dean blew out a breath. "I told her to send Tucker to see me. We got some stuff to iron out, but he's a good boy. He'll make her a good husband. I know they love each other."

Seth nodded in that patient way he had. "That's the most important thing sometimes. Besides, it's not like they'll have to do everything on their own. They've got two families that will help them. It's nice to have two families that can work together like that," Seth said, hoping Dean would get his point.

Dean's eyes locked on Seth's. "Where's Marcus?"

"Gone. He and Lydia got Tessa all settled and then he left. Claire stayed to help, but Marcus left," Seth said.

"Darn! I wanted to thank him."

Seth arched an eyebrow at him. "You know where he lives."

"I'll talk to him tomorrow. I want to see my wife and hold our babies," Dean said with a smile as he took his daughter from Seth. "And I have to tell Tessa about Sadie and Tucker. Tomorrow will be time enough." With the decision made, he disappeared into the bedroom.

CHAPTER 19

C laire knew that Tessa and Dean were going to be fine since Maddie was there to help, so she decided to go home to her husband. She knew Marcus was tired and upset. He'd left with Aiyana as quickly as he could because of the tension that still existed with Dean. She wanted to comfort him. She was so proud of him for everything he'd done to help with the birth of the twins and for taking such good care of Tessa.

Thanks to Marcus, she'd become a better rider and didn't mind traveling alone anymore. She took one of Seth's horses because Marcus had left on Arrow and confidently rode the gelding through the dark. She wasn't afraid of the night anymore and was able to find her way home easily. When she arrived at their house, she found it dark. Marcus must have gone to the camp.

Claire smiled and started on her way. It made sense that he would go there. The camp always made him feel better, and since he'd thought she was staying at the ranch, it was no surprise that he would want to see his other family. When she drew close to the camp, she gave a low whistle as Marcus had taught her. She heard Owl answer and knew it was all right to go on.

When she emerged from the woods, several Indians looked at her and smiled, Wind Spirit among them.

"Hello, sister," she said.

"Hello, sister," Claire responded. Her Lakota still needed some work, but she'd come a long way. "Is my husband here?"

"Yes," Wind Spirit said. "He wanted to offer a sacrifice of thanks for the birth of his niece and nephew. I am not sure exactly where he went."

"That is all right. I will find him," Claire said as she dismounted.

In their tipi, she hurriedly changed into a buckskin dress and came out of the tent. Several of the Indians spoke to her, and she chatted a little with each of them. Black Fox appeared beside her at one point.

"Hello, brother," she said, smiling up at the big Indian.

"Hello, sister. Your Lakota is coming along," he said.

"Thank you."

"Are you looking for Silver Ghost?"

Claire nodded. "Do you know where he is?"

"He went to the ceremonial clearing to give a sacrifice," Black Fox told her.

"Thanks," Claire said and headed there.

SHE HEARD his laugh before she saw him and smiled. Claire wondered what mischief he was up to now. She stepped out of the trees and stopped in her tracks. Marcus was standing with a young maiden who was giggling and teasing him about something.

Claire wasn't close enough to hear exactly what they were saying. She stayed where she was and watched.

"You are so funny, Silver Ghost," Little River told him. "You always make me laugh."

Marcus said, "I am glad."

"And you are handsome," the maiden told him.

He laughed. "And you are flirting, Little River."

"You cannot blame a girl for trying."

"I am flattered, but I am married and you know it," Marcus said.

"You could always have a second wife. I would not mind sharing you."

Marcus laughed. "I think my wife would definitely mind sharing me."

Little River sidled closer to him and ran a hand up one of his arms. "Do you not think I am pretty?"

Marcus took her hand from his arm and said, "Of course you are, but I am not for you. I think some boys in camp would like to court you."

Little River's face fell. "I do not want a boy. I want a man. I want you," she said.

Marcus tried to be kind. "I am sorry, but I love my wife and I am not interested in anyone but her."

Little River wasn't taking him seriously. She grabbed Marcus and kissed him. Marcus was gentle as he pushed her back from him, but his expression was not pleased as he looked at her. A gasp startled them. Marcus looked up to see Claire standing just inside the clearing. She turned and ran back into the trees.

"Darn it, Little River! Look what you have done!" Marcus said. He turned and ran after his wife.

It didn't take him long to catch up with her.

"Claire!" he said as he caught her arm. "Claire, it's not what you think."

She yanked her arm out of his grasp. "How could you do that? I can't believe you!"

"Claire, please let me explain," Marcus said.

"I know what I saw, Marcus. I never thought you would do anything like that," Claire said. "I should have never trusted you. I guess you thought you could just keep up your end of the bargain and have a little something on the side, right?"

"No! Never! I would never cheat on you, Claire!"

Claire broke into sobs. "I loved you, Marcus. I loved you even when other people told me that you weren't reliable or that you were a handful. I married you because I wanted to build a life and a family with you. I can't believe how stupid I was."

She started running again, and Marcus followed her. They burst out of the woods into the camp again. "Claire, please listen to me. Please!"

Everyone watched their progress. When she reached their tipi, Claire stopped and turned to him. Tears streamed from her eyes. "Leave me alone!" she screamed. "I hate you!"

Marcus felt as if she'd dealt him an actual blow. He staggered back a little and didn't follow her into the tipi.

Claire entered their tipi, ripped off her Indian dress, and put her old dress back on. Then she ran to the horse she'd borrowed from Seth and mounted up. She kicked him into action and disappeared back through the trees as Marcus looked on. He would have followed her, but Black Fox said, "Let her go for the night, Marcus. Her temper will cool by tomorrow. Now come and tell us what happened."

Marcus sat down at their fire but refused to tell them the events that had led to the horrible fight.

CLAIRE CRIED the whole way home. She tied the horse to the porch and then went inside. Everywhere she looked, she saw things from the life she and Marcus had shared. She tried to block them out as she went into their room and pulled one of her suitcases from underneath the bed. Tears fell on the clothes that she rammed into it.

In her anguish, she didn't even really know what she was packing. She slammed it shut and took it back out to the porch. Once in the horse's saddle, she leaned down and picked up the suitcase. Then she turned the horse around and galloped away to the ranch.

When she arrived, she banged on Maddie and Seth's door because she didn't want to disturb anyone at the other house. Maddie opened it, dressed in a robe.

"Claire, what's wrong?" she asked.

Claire couldn't answer because she was crying so hard. Maddie guided her inside and sat her down at the kitchen table. She began brewing some tea, then drew a chair close to her sister and held her as her grief poured out.

"He cheated on me!" Claire finally got out.

"Marcus? He cheated on you?" Maddie was shocked.

Claire nodded. "With some Lakota girl. I went home, but he wasn't there and I knew that he'd go to the camp and so I went to find him and when I did, I saw him kissing her and laughing."

Maddie only just managed to keep up with Claire's rambling explanation. "Oh, honey. I'm so sorry." She looked up and saw Seth standing in the doorway. From the grim look on his face, she could tell he'd heard Claire.

Seth and Maddie exchanged a confused look. He would have gone to talk to Marcus, but he didn't know where the Lakota camp was and didn't want to traipse around in the woods all night trying to find him. He figured that he would go to their house the next day and see what he could find out. Eventually, Maddie was able to get Claire calmed down enough to get her to bed.

~

MARCUS DIDN'T SLEEP. He took Aiyana from Wind Spirit and went to his tipi. He put the baby in her cradle and sat near her, humming his daughter to sleep and thinking about how he was going to explain things to Claire in the morning. By the time the sun came up, he had it perfected.

He gathered up his daughter and headed home. When he got there, the house was empty. He noticed some of Claire's clothing on the floor and looked under their bed to confirm his suspicions that she'd packed some things and left.

"C'mon, Aiyana, we're going to go get your mother," he said.

~

MARCUS RODE up the drive and stopped in front of Maddie's house. He whistled Claire's whistle, but she didn't come to the door. He did it again with the same result. His third attempt was met with Maddie coming out of the house.

"Where's my wife?" he asked.

"She doesn't want to see you, Marcus. You should be ashamed of yourself," Maddie said. The disapproval on her face was powerful.

Marcus's eyebrows rose. "I didn't do anything wrong."

"Maybe that sort of thing is all right in Indian culture, but not in ours. Leave her alone, Marcus." Maddie went back into the house and closed the door.

Marcus sat in stunned disbelief.

"Marcus."

He turned to see Seth standing by the barn. His brother motioned to follow him. Inside the barn, Seth led him to a couple of hay bales and they sat down.

"So is it true that you cheated on Claire?" Seth asked bluntly.

"No," Marcus answered.

Seth looked into Marcus's eyes, searching hard for any sign of dishonesty. It was hard to tell with his younger brother since he'd been able to keep so many secrets from his family.

Marcus never flinched or looked away as he said, "Seth, I'm telling you the absolute truth. I didn't cheat on Claire, and I never will."

"So tell me what happened."

"No."

"What do you mean no?"

"I mean no. I'm not going to tell anyone but Claire what happened. This is between me and her, and I'm not going to have anyone play mediator for me. She owes me the courtesy of at least hearing me out," Marcus answered.

"Marcus, I can understand, but maybe I can help the both of you," Seth reasoned.

Marcus shook his head. "All I'll say is that I didn't do anything wrong and leave it at that. I can see she's already told her version of the story and that's fine. That's her choice to do so, but I'm not going to tell anyone but her mine."

Seth watched Marcus march from the barn with Aiyana still on his back. "Darn."

～

MARCUS CAME to the ranch and requested to see Claire every day. She heard her special whistle but never came out to talk to him. The hurt was too deep and she just couldn't face him. She remembered her conversation with Marcus on the night he'd told his family about his heritage. And she remembered that he'd had a child with another woman.

Doubts crowded her mind. Maybe she wasn't enough for him. Maybe she didn't match up to Redtail. They'd started their marriage based on a lie. They'd made a deal and, for him, that's all it had been. She'd been so blinded by his charm and wit that she hadn't seen him for what he really was; a man who hadn't been ready to settle down but had to out of desperation. He'd needed someone to help him raise his daughter and to warm his bed whenever it was convenient for him.

She was miserable, and Maddie's heart broke for her. Seth had tried to get Marcus's side, but his brother stuck to his guns and wouldn't reveal anything except to say that he hadn't done anything wrong. The problem was that she missed him so much. There were times when she considered going back, but she knew she couldn't because her trust in him was broken.

Claire had to admit one thing about Marcus; he never kept Aiyana from her. Seth would bring her to stay with them for a day or so, but it killed Claire when she had to give her back to Marcus. Seth and Maddie were caught between loyalty to Claire and loyalty to Marcus and they tried to not take sides, especially as they hadn't heard Marcus's version of the story.

Marcus took to writing her letters and leaving them on the porch for her. The letters entreated her to at least listen to him. He never used Aiyana as a weapon, however. Claire had to give him credit for that, as well. At night, she lay in her bed and yearned to feel his arms around her, but then she would see him kissing that girl in her mind and her heart would break all over again.

Marcus took to staying at the Lakota camp because he couldn't bear to stay in the home they'd created together. Black Fox and He Who Runs were increasingly worried about him. The only time he smiled was when he was playing with Aiyana. When she was sleeping or with one of her uncles or aunts, he practiced wrestling with the other braves. His anger and hurt were channeled into his fighting, and he became almost lethal in his skill.

With his high intelligence, he was able to figure out the best way to use torque, angle, and speed to achieve maximum pain and to take down his opponent in the least amount of time. It got so that other men wouldn't face him any longer. He stopped bothering to go to the ranch because it was apparent to him that Claire wasn't going to budge.

SETH WAS CONCERNED about Marcus's absence. It wasn't like him to not bring the baby to see Claire. After four days without seeing him, Seth went looking for him. When he didn't find Marcus at his house, he figured that he must be at the Lakota camp. He wasn't quite sure where it was, but he needed to find it and make sure Marcus was well.

He had seen Marcus ride out of the woods at the back of his house and thought it was as good a place to start as any. The trail was narrow, but Hank was able to fit through the foliage. Seth was at home out on the prairies, but the woods were another matter. He began to feel more and more claustrophobic the further along he went. If it hadn't been such a serious situation, he might have turned back.

The trail split and Seth was undecided about which branch he should take. He finally chose the right fork and urged Hank forward again. He estimated that he'd ridden two miles or so and hadn't found anything.

"I must have come the wrong way," he said. He went to turn Hank around and was confronted by two braves that he didn't recognize. "Hi, fellas."

His greeting was met by silence. "Just my luck. I run into ones that don't know English." They just stared at him, and Seth began getting angry. "I'm looking for Silver Ghost." Silence again met his statement. "The heck with this," he muttered.

Slowly, he began walking Hank in the direction he'd been going. He turned every so often and saw that the braves were following him. Seth wasn't going to keep messing around. He pulled Hank up and acted like he'd heard something off in the woods. When the braves turned to look, he put his heels to Hank and the big gelding leaped forward. There was shouting behind him, but he didn't stop. He rode low over Hank's neck, making himself as small as he could. Hank's long legs carried Seth so fast that they soon left the braves behind.

Suddenly, they burst out into a huge clearing. People scattered as Hank ran through the camp. Seth brought his horse to a skidding stop and shouted, "Does anyone here know English?"

He Who Runs heard the commotion and came running. By the time he got there, Seth had been pulled off of Hank and was lying on the ground at knifepoint. The sight of the big cowboy lying there with his hands up struck He Who Runs as funny. He laughed as he walked up to Seth.

"Hello, brother," he said.

"Hello, brother. Can you get these guys the heck off me?"

"What is in it for me?" He Who Runs asked.

"How about I don't kick your behind when I get up?" Seth said with a grin.

"Big words from a man lying on the ground who looks like a pig about to get stuck," He Who Runs replied.

Seth sighed. "I didn't want to have to do this."

Swiftly, he reached out and grabbed the ankle of the nearest brave and gave it a mighty yank. The brave went down. Seth rolled and got hold of a spear, which he rammed into the stomach of the brave who was holding it. He used his advantage to get to his feet and then pulled his revolver and aimed it at a brave who was about to come at him with a knife. The brave stopped mid-stride.

He Who Runs laughed and said something to the braves in Lakota. He must have told them to stand down because they relaxed. He walked up to Seth and said, "Not bad for a cowboy. You are in no danger, Stone Face."

Seth lowered the gun and holstered it. "Stone Face?"

He Who Runs held out his hand in greeting. "Yes. That is your Lakota name. If you could have seen the look on your face as you fought just now, you would understand."

Seth accepted the outstretched hand and shook it. "Stone Face, huh? I kind of like that." Then he moved closer to He Who Runs, hooked a foot around the brave's ankle, and pushed him over backward. He Who Runs landed on his rear with a surprised look on his face.

"You shoulda had your fellas just let me up. If you had, that wouldn't have happened," Seth said with a smile.

Black Fox came up to Seth and looked at He Who Runs. "I keep trying to tell him that White men are tricky," he said with a laugh.

He Who Runs got up and dusted himself off. Smiling, he said, "You win this time, but we will fight again."

"Looking forward to it," Seth said. "Now, where's our brother?"

MARCUS WAS STANDING on the rock ledge where he'd proposed to Claire, looking down at the river. Aiyana was with Eagle Woman, the wife of He Who Runs. He heard footsteps come up behind him and turned to see Seth approaching.

"Hey, little brother," he said.

"Hey, Seth. I see you found the camp," Marcus said. He noticed that Seth's clothes were dusty. "What happened?"

Seth shrugged. "Just a little horseplay."

Marcus gave him a small smile. "I told you that would start at some point."

"So you did. When are you comin' to the ranch again?" Seth asked bluntly. His gaze roamed over Marcus and he barely recognized his brother. Marcus was wearing a loincloth that exposed more of his body than Seth could ever remember seeing. His hair was a little longer and tousled, and Seth was further worried by the haunted look in Marcus's eyes and his lack of curiosity about the impromptu wrestling match. Normally, Marcus would've wanted to know all the details.

"What's the point? There's nothing there for me anymore."

"How about your family? Your wife?"

Marcus made a sarcastic sound. "A wife who won't talk to me? Who doesn't believe in me? And a brother who doesn't want anything to do with me even though I helped his children come into this world and saved his wife's life? Maddie doesn't believe me, and I'll bet Tessa doesn't either. I'll bet even you don't."

"I never said I don't believe you. How can I believe or not believe you when you won't even tell me your story? I need more facts, as you always used to say."

"I've already told you why I won't tell you."

"Okay. So you're going to be stubborn and so is she. Well, things will never work out that way. Do you love her?"

Marcus focused intently on Seth. "Of course I do. I've been doing nothing but showing her how much I love her since I married her. But none of that seems to matter now. She told me she hated me, Seth. Do you know what it's like to have your wife tell you she hates you?"

"No. I don't. We all say stupid stuff when we're mad. She was just upset. At least keep bringing Aiyana to see her."

"Why? What kind of life is that for Aiyana to be carted back and forth between her parents all the time? No, she needs a stable home," Marcus said.

Seth was trying to keep his cool. "Then do me a favor and come check on Tessa and the twins. Dean Junior – D. J. – had a fever the other day. Will you do that much? For me? For Tessa? I know she'd feel better if you checked them out."

Marcus weighed that in his mind. He loved Tessa and wouldn't want her in distress over his nephew. Besides, if the boy was coming down with something, it was better to head it off before it became worse. "All right, but I'm not bothering to change."

Seth grinned. "Come as you are. You'll give everyone something to talk about."

The ghost of a smile stole over Marcus's face and then was gone. "Let's go get it over with, but I'm not taking Aiyana. She can stay here."

"Marcus–" Seth started.

"It's not open for discussion," Marcus cut in. He started walking back to the camp.

∼

As they left the camp, Marcus whistled for Roscoe and the dog followed the two men along on the trail.

Marcus said, "Roscoe is half wolf."

"I know," Seth replied.

"You knew?" Marcus said.

"All you gotta do is look at him close to see it," Seth said. "You act like you're the only one who's ever seen a wolf."

"Okay. I'm glad it doesn't bother you."

Seth sighed and stayed silent the whole way back to the ranch.

CHAPTER 20

arcus rode up the drive without even looking at Seth's house. There was no point. He dismounted and went straight to Dean's house. He entered and stopped in the kitchen of his childhood home, inhaling the familiar scents, and had to steel himself against the flood of emotions that washed over him. Memories of cooking for the family entered his mind, and he had to close his eyes for a moment to get control.

"Tessa?" he called out. "Are you in here?"

"Marcus? In the bedroom," she called back.

When Marcus came into the room, Tessa's eyes widened in surprise at the sight of him in a loincloth and nothing else. She wasn't sure what to think.

Her apprehension amused him and he smiled a little. "Do you like my new outfit?"

"Um, it certainly is unique," she said.

"Is that D. J.?" He gestured at the child in her arms.

"Yes."

Marcus came to stand before her and held out his arms. "Seth said he had a fever the other day and wanted me to check him out."

Tessa handed D. J. over but gave Marcus an odd look. "He's been completely fine. Neither of the twins has had a fever."

Marcus smiled at D. J., and Tessa saw some of the Marcus she knew. "Yeah, you seem fine. I think your Uncle Seth pulled a fast one on me to get me here," he said to the baby. "Seth is tricky. He knows that I can't resist helping people, and he used it on me."

"Did you see Claire?" Tessa asked.

"No, and I don't expect to. She's obviously made up her mind about me," Marcus said.

Tessa's sympathy showed on her face. "Marcus, have you told her you love her?"

Marcus gave her a hard stare. "I've shown her every day how much I love her."

"But have you said the words, Marcus? Women need to hear the words," Tessa explained.

Marcus thought about it for a few moments, then gave D. J. back to his mother.

"If she ever decides to talk to me, I'll tell her," he said.

Tessa sighed and sat back in her chair to rock D. J.

Marcus ran into Seth as he was leaving. "Don't try to trick me like that again, Seth."

Seth tried to stop him, but Marcus pushed past him and mounted his horse. He looked over at Seth's house for a few moments, then galloped away.

SETH CAME out of the barn a couple of days later and was surprised to see Black Fox and Wind Spirit in the drive.

"Hey there," he said with a smile. "What brings you?"

The Indians came forward to greet him. Black Fox said, "Wind Spirit wishes to speak with Fawn."

"Okay. Come on with me."

Black Fox didn't mind houses, but Wind Spirit was a little hesitant until Black Fox reassured her it was safe. Seth entered their parlor and shouted, "Honey, we have company!"

Maddie came from upstairs and stopped for a moment when she saw the Lakota couple in the house. She recognized Black Fox but hadn't met Wind Spirit before.

"Welcome, brother, sister," she said. "Please sit. I'll make some tea."

"Thank you, but I need to speak with Fawn, with Claire," Wind Spirit said. "It is very important."

"She's upstairs. I'll get her," Seth said. He went to the bottom of the stairs and hollered up for her.

Claire appeared at the top of the stairs. "Yes?"

"You have company and no, it's not Marcus," Seth said.

When Claire came down the stairs and saw Black Fox and Wind Spirit, tears filled her eyes because she was so happy to see them. She embraced each of them.

"Fawn, you need to know what happened the night you saw Silver Ghost and that maiden."

Claire's expression became mutinous. "I already know what happened. I saw it with my own eyes," Wind Spirit said, coming straight to the point.

In Lakota, Black Fox said, "Sometimes we do not truly understand what we are seeing, Fawn. The maiden herself told others what happened. Marcus will not tell anyone but you because he believes that as his wife, you should be the one he discusses this with. He will not change his mind about that, as you know."

Wind Spirit nodded. "The girl you saw him with, Little River, is known to be a little wild. She has liked Silver Ghost for a while and thought she would go after what she wanted. She said that she made advances toward him, but he said that he was married and only wanted you. Little River would not take no for an answer and kissed him. She said that he was gentle in pushing her away, but he did push her away."

Black Fox nodded. "That is the whole story. You must do what you think is right. We will leave you to think about things, but I will tell you this, he is not the same man without you. The only joy we ever see on his face now is because of his daughter. I am sure you feel much the same. Goodbye, Fawn."

"Goodbye and thank you," Claire said vaguely. She walked away from them, a little dazed.

Seth followed her. "Claire, what did they say?"

She turned and leaned against him. Seth held her as she cried and haltingly told him what Black Fox and Wind Spirit had told her.

THE WIND PICKED up and made Marcus's hair blow around his face. Thunder rumbled close by, but he didn't flinch. He stood out on his rock ledge with his hands held up to the sky as the rain began pouring down upon him. Lowering his hands, he swept his soaking hair back from his face. The cool water felt refreshing, and he remembered how he used to bathe in the stream at the back of their house knowing that Claire was watching.

Memories of how he'd hurried into the house and taken her in his arms crashed down on him along with the next boom of thunder, and his tears mingled with the rain that ran in rivulets down his face. He stepped back and sat on the ground as his anguish became too much and he gave in to it. He'd never guessed that he would marry the snooty, rich girl from Pittsburgh and fall in love with her.

As he had gotten to know her, he'd found the sweet, loving young woman that Seth had told him about. She was still obstinate and opinionated, but he'd come to understand that it was how she hid her insecurities. In Claire, he'd found a woman who incited a passion in him that he'd never known before. He lived to make her smile and laugh.

He'd lost one of his brothers, but having Claire in his life had helped to ease some of that pain and had given him the strength to go on and not be bitter. His daughter was now the only light in his life. None of his other brothers, his sister, nor anyone could reach his heart anymore. Marcus knew he'd changed, and it wasn't for the better; he couldn't find those easy smiles or the will to pull pranks.

When people needed medical attention, he still treated them, but everyone noticed his grief-dulled eyes and lack of humor as he went about his work. Gone were the comforting smiles and smart remarks designed to draw a laugh or put one at ease. Most of the time, he exhibited a cool detachment, but his hot anger could be triggered by the smallest thing.

Marcus's tears slowed, and he lifted his head again. He rose from the ground and turned to go back to the camp and get his daughter. Claire was standing at the entrance to the trail. A sledgehammer of conflicting emotions hit him and he felt his breathing stop for several moments. He didn't move, but he eyed her with suspicion and anger.

Claire had seen Marcus stand and turn. The way he looked at her was scary. She almost didn't recognize him. There was no smile on his attractive features. His eyes were cold silver orbs instead of the warm gray ones she knew and loved. He was a little more muscular than she remembered, and the loincloth he was wearing emphasized his lean hips and powerful legs.

She had no idea what to say as she walked toward him with slow steps. It was hard, but she held his gaze. When she got within four feet of him, he neatly side-stepped her and started toward the trail. She couldn't believe it. He'd just ignored her, dismissed her as if she didn't matter.

"Marcus! Marcus! Stop!" she said, walking after him.

His long strides ate up the ground and she had to trot to catch up to him. She grasped his arm and tried to make him stop. Suddenly, he whirled around and caught her arm in a painful grip. "What?" he shouted. "What do you want, Claire?"

In all the arguments they'd ever had, Marcus had never used such a harsh tone with her. His rage-filled expression frightened her, and she shrank from him.

He shook her slightly. "What do you want?"

"I came to talk to you," she said finally.

"About?"

"Us."

He laughed cruelly in her face. "Us? There is no *us*, Claire. You've made that perfectly clear to me."

She winced as his grip on her arm tightened even more. Marcus registered the expression and released her. He let her go, not only because he had no desire to hurt her physically but also because touching her was torture.

Claire pressed on. "I know, and I'm so sorry. I'm sorry I didn't believe you, and I'm so sorry that I wouldn't talk to you. I was so hurt, and I was so sure of what I saw."

Marcus's eyes narrowed. "If you were so sure of what you saw, what made you change your mind?"

"Wind Spirit and Black Fox told me. Little River told them what happened," Claire explained.

His nostrils flared and his jaw clenched so hard that Claire thought his teeth would crack. He turned and slammed his fist into a tree, and Claire stepped back from him a little. He looked at her again. "So you took the word of someone who wasn't your husband instead of talking to me about it?"

Claire didn't say anything.

He came closer again. This time, Claire held her ground. "I begged you to listen to me, Claire. Pleaded and appealed to you in every way I could, and you never even had the guts to talk to me face to face and get the facts from me. You're no better than Dean! Neither of you could see the truth about me. I'm just some stupid Indian who can't be trusted, is that it?"

"No! I never thought that!" Claire shouted. "I've never cared about your Lakota heritage and you know that! I love that part of you. It's part of what makes you, you."

His mouth twisted in a snarl. "No, you just told me you hated me, and I never saw you again until now. Not only that, but you turned everyone else but Seth against me. Through all of this, he's the only one who believed in me and stuck by me. I thought you believed in me. I thought you loved me enough to listen to me. I was wrong about that with Dean and I sure as heck was wrong about it with you!"

Claire's eyes began to blaze with her own anger. "I was so angry and upset. I didn't mean it. I do love you. I've never stopped loving you. Please listen to me, Marcus. I'm trying to apologize."

He crossed his arms over his chest in a gesture that told her that he was going to be especially difficult. "What is it you're apologizing for, Claire? There are quite a few things it could be. Let's see; lack of trust in me, telling me you hate me, abandoning our daughter, taking someone else's word over mine? Which is it?"

"All of the above, except that I did not abandon Aiyana. You stopped bringing her."

"I was not about to keep carting her back and forth between us when you wouldn't even take her from my arms and place her back in them. You were a coward, Claire! You hid behind your sister or anyone else who happened to be around just so you didn't have to see me! There was no way that I was going to continue to subject myself or Aiyana to that. Every time I took her back, she cried for you, Claire," Marcus said.

Claire's tears flowed as guilt filled her heart. "I never meant to hurt either of you and I certainly didn't want to cause Aiyana any grief."

"Well, guess what?" Marcus's voice cracked. "You did. You broke my heart, Claire. I fell in love with you. I've never fallen in love with anyone before, and I thought you were the one person in this world who would never break my heart."

Claire blinked as she took in what he'd just said. "You love me?"

"Yes!" he shouted.

"You never told me."

His fist clenched, and she thought he was going to punch a tree again. Even in the emotionally charged situation, she was fascinated with the way his muscles moved and she couldn't deny how much she wanted him.

"I *showed* you every minute of every day. Everything I did was for you and Aiyana. Couldn't you tell? Cooking, reading together, taking care of her together. Teaching you to ride, you teaching me French, laughing together! Couldn't you tell how much I loved you every time we touched and kissed?" he demanded.

"I thought I could but then I saw you with her and I started to wonder if it was all something I had just made up in my head. That you were having fun playing house with me but still wanted other women," Claire said.

He tapped the ring on his left hand. "Do you see this? I take what this means dead serious. Commitment. I know people don't think I'm capable of it, but I've been committed to the people around me all my life, in both families! They just never looked close enough to see it! I've always been good enough to babysit, cook, chop wood, train horses, drive cattle, or fix any darn thing that ever needed fixing, but I'm not good enough to trust or forgive?" He drew himself up and, in a quieter voice, said, "I'm done with all that. I'll raise my daughter and live my life the way I want to live it now. For myself and for her. Go home, Claire. Go home to Pittsburgh where you belong. You don't belong here."

Claire was stunned. "But we're married."

"I know it's not very fashionable in your circles, but we'll get a divorce since an annulment is out of the question. The marriage was consummated, so it'll have to be a divorce," Marcus said. "I'll sign it whenever it's ready."

Now Claire crossed her arms. "So you're ready to throw everything away?"

"Ha! You were! Can you tell me that you would have sought me out if Wind Spirit hadn't told you what happened?" Marcus said.

"Yes, I would have."

"When?"

Claire threw her arms up. "I don't know! I don't think I would have been able to stand it much longer! I was in agony without you. I've been just as miserable as you have."

She closed the distance between them and touched his chest. A muscle jumped under her hand. "I love you, Marcus. I need you and

I want you. I regret more than you'll ever know that I hurt you. But somehow, I'll make it up to you."

Claire's touch was having a powerful effect on him. He stepped back, but she went with him. He kept going until he backed into a tree. She had him trapped. Once she'd started, Claire couldn't stop touching him.

"Claire, don't. I can't do this," he said.

"Do what?" Claire asked. She slid her hands around his back.

Marcus reined in his ardor for her. "Is that your plan? Have you come to seduce and win me back with your feminine wiles?"

"No. That wasn't in my plan, but is it working?" Claire asked.

"Yes, but not in the way you want. Not emotionally," Marcus said.

Claire withdrew her hands from him. "Very well. I can see that you're not ready yet, but I'm going to wait until you are. I love you. If you let me, I swear I'll spend every day showing you how much I love you, and I'll never doubt you again. You know where you can find me."

Claire walked past him, leaving him standing on the trail. He watched her leave and then went back to the rock ledge.

CHAPTER 21

$\mathcal{W}$ ord of Claire's confrontation with Marcus spread through the ranch. She told Maddie almost everything that had happened and about how Marcus felt like everyone had turned their backs on him. Dean became angry when he heard, but his anger was self-directed. A couple of days after Claire had talked to Marcus, Dean went to talk to Seth. He found him checking on some fencing in the north pasture.

As Dean walked up to him, Seth smiled and said, "Hey, Dean."

"Where's the darn Indian camp?" Dean asked.

"What?" Seth asked.

"Are you hard of hearing? Where's the camp?" Dean repeated.

"Why?"

"I want to go there," Dean said. "That's usually why someone asks where something is."

"Okay. You don't have to be like that about it. It just surprises me that you wanna go there. Why do you?"

"It's time for me to talk to Marcus. Maybe I can make him see that he can't throw his happiness with Claire away. I understand why both of them were hurt, but I'm sure they can work it out. As far as he and I go, I don't know if it's possible to work things out between us now, but I'm gonna try."

Seth tipped his hat back so he could see Dean better. After looking at him for a few moments he said, "Well, it's about darned time. C'mon, let's go. It'll be easier to show you. Besides, if they don't know you, they might kill you."

Dean started back toward the ranch. "That's what guns are for, Seth."

Seth laughed and followed his brother.

~

WHEN THEY WERE close to the camp, Seth let out a low whistle and was answered with a night owl call. He smiled. "That's Owl's call. He's Marcus's older brother by one year. Looks a lot like Marcus."

"Oh, yeah. I remember him from the wedding," Dean replied. "So how often do you come here?"

"A couple of times a week, I guess. I've been keeping tabs on Marcus. And I like to heckle He Who Runs."

They left the woods, and Dean looked around the huge clearing. He'd never seen so many Indians in one place. He was surprised when some of them smiled at Seth, and more so when a little boy flew at him. Seth picked him up and threw him in the air.

"Raven! How are you, boy?" Seth said as he held on to the little boy.

Dean thought the boy looked a few years older than Mikey. His dark eyes shone as he smiled at Seth.

"Good, Stone Face." Raven put his arms around Seth's neck and squeezed.

Seth hugged him back and then put him down. "Where's your *niyate*?"

Dean looked at Seth. "Are you learning their language?"

"Some. I'm picking up words here and there. The easy ones. Black Fox is Raven's pa."

"Come," Raven said, motioning for them to follow.

They followed the boy until they stopped in front of a tipi. Dean recognized Black Fox.

Black Fox looked at Dean and said, "I think the heavens will open again today because you have come to visit." He smiled to show he was joking. "Welcome, brother."

"Thanks," Dean said. He was uncomfortable and didn't know what he was supposed to say. "Where's Marcus?"

Seth frowned at him. "Nothin' like gettin' right to the point. Don't mind him."

"Silver Ghost is probably where he spends most of his time," Black Fox said. "Stone Face knows where that is."

Dean looked at Seth. "Stone Face?"

"It's my Lakota name. They'll have to find one for you," Seth explained.

"I like my own name just fine," Dean said. "Thanks for the information, Black Fox. Lead on, Seth."

"I'll be back in a bit," Seth said. "Then I can tell you some stories about Dean."

"You better not," Dean threatened.

Seth laughed and headed for Marcus's hideout. Dean followed him through the clearing. Every so often, someone would talk to Seth and Dean wondered exactly how often Seth had really been coming to the camp. He seemed awfully friendly with them. He noticed a few of the women eying Seth with speculation. Seth tipped his hat to a couple of them, and they laughed.

"Seth!" Dean said, "What's the matter with you?"

Seth laughed. "Aw, Dean, it's just harmless fun. They all know I'm madly in love with my wife. I've had a few try to change my mind about that, but I got my point across. So don't worry."

Dean was surprised when one woman looked at him in the same way. He gave her a small smile and then turned his eyes to the ground. Seth entered the woods and Dean said, "Where the heck are we going?"

"To find little brother. He's most likely down this trail. He has a really pretty spot where he likes to sit and think," Seth answered.

After a few minutes, the trail widened and opened up to reveal a panoramic view of the river. Dean saw that they were far above the valley. Then he caught sight of Marcus sitting on a huge rock ledge that jutted out over the water. As they walked forward, Marcus heard them and turned around.

He saw Seth and gave him a little smile. When he saw Dean, he shook his head in surprise and got to his feet.

"What's wrong?" he asked. "Is it Tessa? The twins?"

"No, they're fine," Seth reassured him. "Why do you think something's wrong?"

Marcus pointed at Dean. "That's the only reason he would ever come here."

"Marcus, everyone's fine except for me and your wife," Dean said.

"What do you mean?" Marcus asked.

"That's my cue to leave," Seth said. "You fellas sort things out and then come get me. I'm gonna see if I can beat He Who Runs at that bones game again."

They watched Seth walk off, then Dean said, "C'mon, sit down with me."

Once they were settled, Dean looked out over the river valley. The sound of the river after the heavy rain was a soft roar. The sky was a vivid blue backdrop to the green foliage. "I can see why you come here, Marcus. It's a pretty place."

"Yeah. It is. It's where I proposed to Claire."

"It is? I didn't know that."

"What do you want, Dean?" Marcus asked tiredly.

"There's a lot of things I could say to that, but although it all goes together, it boils down to one thing; I want my little brother back," Dean said.

Marcus put his head on his knees and began to laugh. It wasn't the rich, easy laugh that Dean remembered so well. Instead, it was a sharp, angry sound.

"What are you laughing at?" Dean asked with a frown.

"You. Claire. Everyone," Marcus replied.

"Explain that."

Marcus looked at Dean, and Dean didn't know what to make of the man sitting next to him. Bitterness showed in the lines around his mouth and the coldness in his eyes.

"I'm good enough when people finally decide I am. When they're ready for me, not when I'm ready for them."

Dean sighed. "Please, Marcus. No riddles."

"Okay. No riddles. Why am I suddenly good enough for you now? You threw me out of your house after I bared my soul to you. You put my daughter's safety in jeopardy when you swiped everything off the counters. I forgave you, Dean, and I came to you as your brother and asked you to do one darn thing for me on the most important day of my life, outside of finding out about Aiyana.

"But no. You couldn't get past your pride to do even that much for me. I helped your twins come into this world and made sure that Tessa was all right even though I knew how you felt about me. I put that aside and helped you and your family because, despite how much you've hurt me, I still love you."

Dean held Marcus's gaze and said, "You're right, Marcus. I should have never done that to you. I regret not standing with you so much. I didn't get a chance to thank you the night the twins were born. I was talking to Sadie out in the barn and when I got back to the house, you were already gone. I can't tell you how much it meant to me. To us."

Marcus nodded. "You're welcome."

"You wanna know what I was talking to Sadie about?" Dean said.

"Sure."

"I'm gonna be a grandfather in about six months."

Marcus's head whipped around. "What?"

Dean laughed. "Yep. Sadie's pregnant. Tucker asked her to marry him. I've had a talk with him and we have an understanding."

Marcus laughed, and this time, it sounded like the old Marcus. "You're gonna be a grandfather and you just had twins!" he spluttered, and then was overtaken with laughter again.

"Shut up, Marcus. It's not funny," Dean said.

Marcus nodded that it was.

"Okay, maybe it's a little funny," Dean conceded.

"It's a lot funny," Marcus said. "Oh, now my gut hurts. I haven't laughed like that in a long time."

"I'm glad that I can amuse you," Dean said with a scowl.

"You sure can."

Dean sobered. "Marcus, I know that I've been a real buzzard. The day Seth and the women got back from Pittsburgh, we saw you jumping Rosie over the barbed-wire fence and it ticked me off."

"Oh. Yeah, you were always telling me not to do that. I'm too reckless, too childish and all that," Marcus said sarcastically.

"Do you know why I've always tried to get you to be safer? Because I love you and I didn't want you to get hurt or killed. You're my little brother and I've always looked out for you. When Pa was dying, he made me promise that I would take care of you and Ma. I swore to him that I would, and I did."

Marcus met Dean's eyes. "I didn't know that."

"I know. But you know me when I make a promise. I keep it, no matter what. So I ragged on you and rode you hard, but it wasn't because I didn't think you weren't capable, it was just because I felt like I had to do it to keep you safe. We lost our parents. I lost Sarah and a baby, and I couldn't lose you or Seth. When he was hurt, I was so scared that we *were* going to lose him."

"Me, too," Marcus admitted.

"I thought I had to take over for Pa. To kind of become a father to you," Dean said. "I think I was probably too hard on you sometimes."

"Probably? You were," Marcus stated clearly.

"I know, but through it all, you just kept smiling and teasing me and I thought you weren't taking me seriously," Dean said. "After what you said the night you asked me to stand with you, I realized that you'd been paying attention all along."

"That's right. I was."

"I know, and it makes me feel good that you learned so much

from me. What doesn't feel good is knowing how much I've let you down lately. See, when I read what happened to Ma, I think I directed some of the anger I felt about it at you. In fact, I know I did." Dean took a deep breath. "Then when you told us that you had this whole other family, I was thrown for another loop. I'm not good with change, Marcus."

"This I know."

Dean ignored his remark. "What you told us completely changed everything I thought I knew about you. It was almost like you'd become a stranger to me and I had no idea who you were anymore. You were half Indian and your other family knew all about us. I was hurt that you hadn't come to me all those years ago because I thought we were close enough that you could have told me anything."

"I was a scared kid, Dean. I was afraid of being rejected, and it seems I was right to be," Marcus said.

Dean put a hand on Marcus's arm. "Marcus, I wouldn't have rejected you back then. I would have been shocked, but I wouldn't have sent you away. The reason I rejected you was because I was hurt that you'd kept secrets from us. I really did think that we were close enough for you to tell me anything at any time. And I was jealous of these people. Still am, but I'm learning that I'm going to have to share you."

Marcus smiled. "You? Jealous?"

"Heck, yeah. You've been *my* little brother longer than you've been *their* little brother and I didn't want you to be anyone's little brother but mine," Dean admitted. "Now that I say it out loud, it sounds childish, but that's how I felt."

"I will never stop being your little brother, Dean. You know, Seth asked me if I loved my Lakota family more than you guys," Marcus said.

"What did you say?" Dean asked.

"That I have enough love for all of you. I love you all for different reasons. My relationship with each of my siblings is different. Seth is the brother who got me drunk for the first time and caroused with me sometimes when I got old enough. You're the brother that I look up to kind of like a father. Black Fox is the brother who taught me how to throw knives and walk silently. He Who Runs is steady like you. He's a great family man and very responsible. We wrestle all the time. He's the one who taught me how to fight. Owl is the brother that I can really clown around with. His personality is a lot like mine. My sister and I are close, too."

"How do you keep everyone straight?" Dean asked with a laugh. "It must be that big brain of yours."

"I guess."

"Marcus, don't stay mad at Claire too long. She loves you. Heck, she's loved you since she first met you. I saw it then and knew it when she came back here in May. She should have talked to you to get your side of things. I should have, too. I knew that you didn't cheat on her," Dean said.

"How did you know that?" Marcus said.

"Because you said that you learned how to be a good husband from me and I've never cheated on either of my wives. So I figured that since you'd learned that from me, you'd never do that to Claire." Dean gave Marcus a sideways hug and kissed the side of his head. "Here's another lesson I'm going to teach you. Forgiveness. I forgive you for not telling us for so long. I know why you didn't, now. I also forgive you for kicking my behind the way you did."

Marcus laughed. "I wish you could have seen your face that day. It was priceless."

"I'm sure it was. Can you forgive me?" Dean asked, looking into Marcus's eyes.

One crack in Marcus's heart began to knit together, and he smiled at Dean. "Yeah. I can forgive you."

"Thanks, little brother." Dean thumped his shoulder and got to his feet. "Now I expect to see you first thing tomorrow. We've got a last hay crop to bring in and I need your help. And put some clothes on, for God's sake."

As Dean walked toward the trail, Marcus's warm laughter followed him.

CHAPTER 22

*C*laire lay in bed one night watching the shadows on the wall from the oak tree outside. The wind was blowing, and it seemed as if another storm was on the way. She was just getting drowsy when she heard something outside. It sounded like a bird. The sound came again and she bolted up in bed. She had to be sure. The third time she heard it, she got out of bed and ran to the window.

Marcus was standing beneath the window gazing up. He must have seen her because he waved and then gestured for her to come to him. She didn't bother putting anything else on besides her night-gown. She was in too much of a hurry to get to him. Carefully, she went down the stairs, trying not to make any noise.

When her feet touched the parlor floor, she ran to the door, opened it quietly, and shut it behind her. When she turned around, Marcus was right behind her. She jumped at the sight of him, and he put a hand over her mouth to stifle any noise that might come from it. He smiled at her and let his hand drop, then looked down at her feet and silently asked why she didn't have any shoes on.

Claire thought it was an odd thing to be worried about and shrugged. He rolled his eyes and made walking motions with his fingers. Claire just shrugged again. Marcus frowned at her and then shrugged, too. He picked her up and carried her down the steps to where Rosie and Arrow were waiting. He put her up on Rosie, then mounted Arrow and motioned for her to follow him.

She whispered to him, "Yes, Marcus. I know to follow you. I'm not going to sit here on this horse in the drive all night."

Marcus leaned over and muffled his laughter in Arrow's mane. Claire had trouble stifling her own laugh. When they were a safe distance from the ranch, Marcus dropped back to ride beside her.

"Hi, Claire," he said.

"Hi, dummy," she said.

He laughed. "I don't think I've ever heard of anyone using the word *dummy* as a term of endearment before."

"So, what do you want, Marcus?" she asked.

"You. I want you. I want us back. Claire, I love you so much. I've never cheated on you and I never will. You're the only woman I want to be with. You're my wife and the mother of my baby and hopefully more to come. Can you forgive me?" he asked.

Claire looked at him as the wind caught his hair and the moonlight glinted off his eyes. "Can you forgive me for not trusting you enough?"

"I already have."

"Me too."

Marcus's brows drew together. "You've already forgiven yourself?"

"No! You! I've forgiven you."

He laughed. "I knew what you meant."

"It's good to hear your laugh again. *Your* laugh. I didn't like the other Marcus. He's scary," Claire admitted.

Marcus nodded. "Yeah, I didn't like him much either. It sure didn't feel good being him. I'm sorry he scared you. I don't ever want him to come back again."

"Me neither. Although, I wouldn't mind if you wore his clothes. He looked very delicious in them. Especially standing there in the rain like that," she said.

No sooner were the words out of her mouth than Marcus hauled her off Rosie and sat her in front of him on Arrow. His mouth covered hers and his hands were everywhere. She enthusiastically reciprocated his actions. Arrow wasn't sure what was going on and shifted on his feet. Marcus didn't stop kissing Claire as he slid off the horse, pulling her with him.

He picked her up again so her bare feet wouldn't get hurt by the stones, then ran into the field beside the road. Claire giggled as he laid her down on the grass and started removing his shirt. Her laughter grew as he fumbled with the buttons.

"I hate clothes!" he shouted, giving up on the buttons and ripping the shirt open.

"If you keep doing that, we're going to have to get you more shirts or more buttons. I'm not sure which," she said.

"Okay. I don't care. More shirts, buttons, whatever," he said. When he was finally free of the hated garment, he lay down beside her, drew her hand to his hair, and said, "Pull."

And she did.

EPILOGUE

$\mathcal{A}$t the end of October, Dean walked Sadie down the aisle of the church. Tucker Foster fidgeted as Sadie got closer, but his eyes never left her. He was a good-looking young man with dark hair and blue eyes.

As he escorted Sadie, images of Sadie growing up assailed Dean. Her birth and the first time he'd held. He'd been happy and terrified all at once. Then the next thing he'd known, she'd been a toddler and always on the move. He remembered first teaching her to ride a horse and, later on, to drive a buggy. She'd become a competent cook and knew all about childcare. She was skilled at domestic pursuits and had absorbed a lot of educational knowledge from Tessa and Marcus. And he remembered the day he'd found out Sarah was pregnant. He was incredibly proud of her.

He looked over at her and saw Sarah in her and knew that Sadie's mother was with them that day. When they reached the altar, Dean gave Tucker that look that all fathers seem to instinctively know, the one that says *If you hurt my daughter in any way, shape, or form, I'll kill you.* Then he handed his little girl over to the young man. He kissed Sadie's cheek and went to sit with Tessa.

His wife took his hand and squeezed hard. He looked at her and saw that she had tears in her eyes, too. Dean kissed her, then bent to kiss little Catherine's head as she rested in her mother's arms. Then he turned to Seth, who was holding D. J., and motioned for him to hand his son to him. Seth shook his head. Dean shot him an insistent look, but Seth still refused.

A hand came from behind Seth and smacked him in the head.

"Give the man his son," Marcus said.

Seth looked around his wife at his brother, who just smiled at him and motioned with his head to do as he'd instructed.

"Will you two behave?" Maddie whispered. "Give the baby to Dean."

Seth frowned but handed his nephew over. Dean smiled and turned back around. Seth gave Marcus a Lakota hand signal that was not very nice. Marcus sent back one of his own, and Seth smiled. Marcus grinned but somehow refrained from laughing as Pastor John began the service. Marcus felt Claire's hand on his arm and turned to her. He'd expected to see a look of reproach on her face. Instead, he saw that she was laughing silently.

He envied her ability to laugh like that. She made no sound but shook so hard that the pew bench creaked a little, and that made it even harder for Marcus not to laugh. He wanted to tell her to stop but knew if he opened his mouth, his laughter would erupt and Dean would disown him again for disrupting his daughter's wedding ceremony. He had to bite the inside of his cheek to hold it back.

Maureen heard the creaking and looked back to see what was causing it. Claire stopped laughing instantly when her mother gave her a stern look. When Maureen looked at Marcus the same way, however, he winked at her. She gave him a tiny smile and then she turned back around.

Everyone's attention became focused on the altar. As the young couple said their vows, Dean and Tessa remembered their own wedding and how scared they'd been. Dean hadn't known he was in love with Tessa at the time, but looking back, he realized that he must have been or he would never have married her.

Tessa had been smarter than him, and she'd told him on more

than one occasion that she could tell that he loved her by the way he said her name and smiled at her. Dean had learned from personal experience that saying it *and* showing it was the best way to get the message across. That way, there could be no mistake. He'd also learned that listening and reserving judgment was a good course of action. When he'd had his talk with Tucker, he'd used his newfound knowledge and heard the young man out. Tucker's devotion to Sadie and their unborn baby had impressed him, and Dean was glad he hadn't gotten angry.

Tessa had learned that following your dreams, even if it meant stepping into the unknown, could reap incredible rewards and that not giving in to doubt could lead to a lifetime of happiness. She looked at each of her five children in turn and wondered where the years had gone.

As someone who'd been so impatient to start her future, Tessa had finally learned that patience was best in some instances. She'd had the patience to wait to hear those magic words from her husband and to see him through a difficult time, even when she didn't approve of his choices. She'd waited and watched him figure out what she'd already known he needed to do.

Though Seth appeared to be a big, tough cowboy most of the time, he was a softie when it came to women and kids. When he'd been hurt, Seth had been taught that letting his softer side show wasn't a sign of weakness. During his recovery in Pittsburgh, he'd learned what true courage was when he'd told Maddie that he loved her and asked for her hand in marriage even though he'd been scared to death. Her refusal had hurt him more deeply than he'd thought anything ever could.

Maddie had learned that sometimes you had to rise above your fears and go after what you want in order to be happy. There were times when it paid to throw caution to the wind and chase your dreams. She'd followed Seth halfway across the country to get her man and beg his forgiveness. Seth had learned another lesson in courage when he'd granted it. They were even happier now than they had been on the day they'd married. Seth looked down at Maddie's growing stomach and into her smiling eyes. Then he reached behind her and patted Marcus's shoulder.

Marcus leaned back and met Seth's eyes. Seth sent him the Lakota sign for *thanks*. Marcus shrugged since he didn't know what Seth meant. Seth signed *baby,* and Marcus signed *you're welcome.* Then they turned back to the service again.

A smile played around Marcus's mouth as he thought about how he still didn't know Claire's middle name. The day they'd said their I do's and he'd uttered the phrase from his "touching and funny" proposal was the day he'd realized that, somehow, he'd fallen in love with her. He'd recently learned that being stubborn and not doing everything in your power to resolve a conflict could rob you of all happiness and turn you bitter. He'd had to learn his own lesson in forgiveness.

When Marcus took her hand, Claire looked at her husband and responded to the wink he gave her with one of her own. Before she'd come to Dawson the second time, she'd been too serious; now she had learned how to laugh and have fun. She'd also learned that communication and trust were the most important elements of any relationship and there was no chance of joy or hope without them. Aiyana began to babble and Claire smiled at their daughter. She wasn't sure yet, but she thought she and Marcus might have another little one before too long.

Sadie had learned all of these lessons from the adults in her life. As she looked into Tucker's eyes and said her vows, she knew that she would use those lessons to help make her and Tucker's life together one filled with happiness and love. They would help get them through the hard times and keep them moving forward until the good times returned.

Jack had learned that you could eat any time you wanted and not have to wait for someone else to do it for you if you knew how to cook for yourself. Since he'd learned to cook, he'd also learned that if you were good at it, other people always wanted you to cook for *them.* Uncle Seth was evidence of this, especially when he was still hungry in the morning.

~

SADIE'S RECEPTION was beautiful and touching. Geoffrey and Seth did not dance together because they knew the Fosters wouldn't have understood the meaning behind it. However, Seth teased Geoffrey mercilessly about becoming a great-grandfather. Marcus danced often with Maureen and told her she was too good-looking to be a great-grandmother.

Since all of their daughters and family were in Dawson, Geoffrey and Maureen were lonely in their Pittsburgh home. After careful consideration, they had decided that Geoffrey should sell his lucrative business interests so they could move out West to be with the rest of their family. They figured that they would spend their golden years learning a new way of life and helping raise all the little ones that were already in their lives and the ones yet to come.

As the Montana moon shone its approving light down on the community center in Dawson, Tessa and Dean watched their daughter and son-in-law dance together for the first time. As the family inside celebrated the new marriage of Mr. and Mrs. Tucker Foster, each of them knew they would never forget all the lessons they had learned. And all of it had been started by one letter sent from the East to the West.

The End

OTHER BOOKS BY LINDA BRIDEY

Montana Mail Order Brides Series

Westward Winds (Montana Mail Order Brides Book 1)

Westward Dance (Montana Mail Order Brides Book 2)

Westward Bound (Montana Mail Order Brides Book 3)

Westward Destiny (Montana Mail Order Brides Book 4)

Westward Fortune (Montana Mail Order Brides Book 5)

Westward Justice (Montana Mail Order Brides Book 6)

Westward Dreams (Montana Mail Order Brides Book 7)

Westward Holiday (Montana Mail Order Brides Book 8)

Westward Sunrise (Montana Mail Order Brides Book 9)

Westward Moon (Montana Mail Order Brides Book 10)

Westward Christmas (Montana Mail Order Brides Book 11)

Westward Visions (Montana Mail Order Brides Book 12)

Westward Secrets (Montana Mail Order Brides Book 13)

Westward Changes (Montana Mail Order Brides Book 14)

Westward Heartbeat (Montana Mail Order Brides Book 15)

Westward Joy (Montana Mail Order Brides Book 16)

Westward Courage (Montana Mail Order Brides Book 17)

Westward Spirit (Montana Mail Order Brides Book 18)

Westward Fate (Montana Mail Order Brides Book 19)

Westward Hope (Montana Mail Order Brides Book 20)

Westward Wild (Montana Mail Order Brides Book 21)

Westward Sight (Montana Mail Order Brides Book 22)

Westward Horizons (Montana Mail Order Brides Book 23)

Dawson Chronicles Series

Mistletoe Mayhem: Book 1

After the Storm: Book 2

Spirit Journey: Book 3

Echo Canyon Brides Series

Montana Rescue (Echo Canyon Brides Book 1)

Montana Bargain (Echo Canyon Brides Book 2)

Montana Adventure (Echo Canyon Brides Book 3)

Montana Luck (Echo Canyon Brides Book 4)

Montana Fire (Echo Canyon Brides Book 5)

Montana Hearts (Echo Canyon Brides Book 6)

Montana Christmas (Echo Canyon Brides Book 7)

Montana Orphan (Echo Canyon Brides Book 8)

Montana Surprise (Echo Canyon Brides Book 9)

Montana Miracle (Echo Canyon Brides Book 10)

Montana Ricochet (Echo Canyon Brides Book 11)

CONNECT WITH LINDA BRIDEY

Visit my website at www.lindabridey.com to sign up to my newsletter so that you will be notified as to when my new releases are available.

Printed in the USA
CPSIA information can be obtained
at www.ICGtesting.com
LVHW090758211023
761736LV00036B/414

9 781500 931681